I0760476

Queens of the Fae book Eleven

FAE'S ENEMY

MELISSA A. CRAVEN

M. LYNN

Edited by Caitlin Haines
Cover by Maria Spada

Chapter One
GULLIVER

"Gulliver! What do you mean, *'don't get mad'?"* The disembodied voice reverberated across the courtyard in a burst of wind. Gulliver flinched, knowing exactly what was coming for him. Familiar power wrapped around his chest, like the tendrils of some unseen vine, squeezing the air from his lungs until he gasped for breath.

It released him, but not before tugging on his tail. His feet skidded across the stone as the magic gave him a final push. A scream ripped from his throat, and he stumbled. As he looked up, he caught the terror in Sophie's eyes. Eavha had just managed to convince her to join them in the courtyard for some fresh air and a simple game of liathroid.

"Heads up, Gullie!" Eavha called, not bothering to pause the game to let him recover his bearings. The ball sailed toward Gulliver, hitting him square in the stomach.

"Oof." He fumbled the ball and scrambled to catch it but was jerked backward again.

"Eavha," he yelled, exasperated with the one queen who was normally his favorite person in all the worlds. "Make her stop."

Annoyance sparked through him when Eavha only laughed. Declan shook his head with an affectionate smile for his favorite person. But Sophie-Ann... she looked horrified. This was exactly the kind of magic he hadn't wanted her to see. She still wouldn't speak to him, and this would only make it worse.

He stumbled toward the open front gates, his tail aching where it met the base of his spine. "Tierney O'Shea," he growled. "You've had your fun, isn't that enough?"

"*Don't get mad?*" Tia said again, this time her voice closer, more dangerous.

Gulliver sighed as the magic pulled him from the courtyard into the wide-open space between the castle and the mostly dead forest surrounding it with twisted and burned trees that would take generations to recover.

He stopped abruptly and would have fallen forward if not for the magic holding him up. His legs wobbled as the unseen force turned him quickly to meet the visitors.

"Don't get mad?" Tia seethed, hands on her hips. "Are you kidding me, Gulliver?"

Her parents stood on either side of her, looking amused in a subdued sort of way. Worry was etched into every line of their faces.

"Erm, nice to see you, Majesties." Gulliver bowed. Brea and Lochlan weren't the king and queen any longer, but he would always see them as such.

"Don't look at them." Tia narrowed her eyes. "They're not the Queen of Iskalt who sent you on a simple information-gathering mission and found you holed up in Lenya, of all places."

He rubbed the back of his neck. "Well, you didn't exactly find me did you? I sent you a note."

"A note." Tia lifted a hand, curling her fingers in so her power took hold of him once more. Only, this time, it propelled him toward her to collide against her in a tight hug. She gripped him as if she'd thought she might never see him again.

"I have been so worried," she whispered, burying her face in his chest.

Gulliver held her, realizing just how much he needed his best friend. They were soulmates, connected in a way he'd never had with anyone else. When she wasn't by his side, he wasn't fully himself. As though he was missing a limb.

"Did you really have to yank me from the courtyard?"

She laughed. "Absolutely. That was the fun part."

"What if I'd been inside? Were you going to pull me through the walls?"

She leaned away and looked up at him. "I hadn't really thought about that."

Lochlan cleared his throat, sliding his arm through Brea's. "Think we could take this inside?"

Gulliver looked back at the castle, where the guards along the wall watched them with open curiosity.

"Tia!" Eavha ran toward them, lifting the bottom of her dress to keep from tripping. The two girls hugged. "You have got to teach me how to do that. Gulliver was all, 'make her stop'! You should have seen his face. It was hilarious."

Gulliver turned away from his diabolical friends as Sheba bound across the distance toward them, looking like she wasn't going to stop. A squeal escaped Gulliver moments before the giant cat reached them. She stopped at Brea's side, staring up at her in expectation.

"Oh." Brea covered her mouth in surprise. "A cat. How precious."

"That's not a cat, my love." Lochlan tried to pull her away, but she didn't budge. "It's much too big."

Brea didn't listen to him as she buried her hands in Sheba's fur. The cat let out a sound somewhere between a purr and a roar.

Lochlan started toward the castle. "Let's get out of this sun before this old ice king melts into a puddle."

Eavha and Tia linked arms and ran after him, leaving Gulliver with Brea and Sheba. Brea fell in step beside him. "Sorry for the dramatic entrance." She sighed. "The moment we stepped out of the portal, Tia took off like a rocket."

He was used to Brea saying human things he didn't understand, so he didn't ask what a rocket was. Her explanations never made much sense anyway. "I guess I should have explained more in my message."

"You don't say?" Brea took his arm as they stepped through the gates. "We have much to discuss. A lot of questions."

They had no idea.

Declan met them in the center of the courtyard.

"Where's ..." Gulliver stopped himself, needing to explain things to Tia before revealing the human girl's presence.

"In her room." Declan's dour expression told Gulliver there was more he wanted to say, but he didn't need to.

Gulliver pictured Sophie's face, the fear, as he flew backward. He'd exposed her to so little magic, but Tia was in no way cautious with her power. He should have known something like this would happen.

"Now that we have our greetings out of the way, is there someplace we can speak privately?" Lochlan clasped his hands behind his back, looking ever the king. Yet, there was something lighter in his stance ever since he'd handed the crown of Iskalt over to his daughter.

Declan nodded. "We've been using the dining hall for meetings of this sort."

"Perfect." Gulliver's stomach rumbled. "Then, we can eat while we talk."

"Some things never change." Tia rolled her eyes to Eavha.

Gulliver shrugged. "A leopard can't change its stripes."

"Spots," Brea whispered, patting him on the back. "Leopards have spots, honey, but nice try."

He wasn't even sure what a leopard was, but he'd grown up hearing Brea say it quite often about her husband.

They crowded together as they entered the quiet castle that now buzzed with activity over the arrival of their visitors.

"Ariella," Eavha called. "Ready two guest rooms."

Ariella hesitated. "Lady Eavha, we only have one more usable room. The—"

Eavha cut her off. "That's right. Our other is occupied. Fine, just the one then. My sister-by-marriage can stay with me. Declan will sleep in the guard's quarters."

"Sleepover! I've seen them in many human movies. But don't we need to find some paint for our nails?" Tia gave her mother a concerned look. "I don't want to do it wrong."

Eavha shrugged. "There might be some left over from the renovations of the east wing."

"That's not quite right, girls." Brea laughed. "I'm not sure there's a fae equivalent of nail polish, but you can do a girl's sleepover without it in a pinch."

"Oh good." Tia giggled.

"Aren't you supposed to be a queen or something?" Gulliver bumped Tia with his shoulder.

She straightened. "Just worry about yourself. You'll see how much of a queen I am soon enough."

He swallowed. That sounded ominous. Sure, he'd failed in his mission, but he had a good reason, and she'd understand as soon as he explained. Tia was well-versed in the healing pools and using them to save the man she loved. She couldn't blame him too much. Could she?

Not that he loved Sophie. The woman wouldn't even speak to him. The thought tugged at his heart, but he tried to ignore it as a servant appeared with a tray of glasses and a flagon of wine.

"No, no. Not the Gelsiberry!" Eavha shrieked and chased them back toward the kitchens, issuing orders.

"Lord Declan?" A soldier walked toward them. "We've received a message from Queen Bronagh."

Declan nodded before turning to the others. "Please, have a seat. I will return shortly."

When he hurried off, it left Gulliver staring at the three O'Sheas. He lowered himself into a chair at the long wooden table, wishing Eavha would hurry up with that wine.

"We have many things to discuss." Lochlan sat beside him. "Tell us of your mission in the human city."

The two women took the chairs across the table from him, and Tia shot an annoyed look at her father. "Dad, I know the whole taking a backseat thing is still new for you, but I'll handle this."

He looked confused for a moment before he gave her a sheepish smile. "Apologies, my little queen." He nodded for her to continue.

Tia reached into the pocket she'd had sewn into of every one of her dresses. She got the idea from her mother's human clothes, stating that if fae were superior beings, they must put pockets in dresses.

Pulling out a folded paper Gulliver instantly recognized as a page from a human newspaper, she slapped it on the table. "Go on. Look at it."

He glanced at each fae in turn. Lochlan was tense, his jaw tight. Brea had tears shining in her eyes. Tia was defiant. It was how she acted when she didn't know what to do.

Fear struck him. For whatever that page said, whatever it would mean.

Slowly, he unfolded it, his eyes swimming over lines and lines of text but he couldn't absorb a single word. The pictures took his attention. Two of them were side by side, blurry but recognizable.

Toby and Griff stared back, warning him that whatever he was about to read would shift the axis of his world.

"What was Griff doing in the human world long enough to cause trouble?" Lochlan asked.

"He came ..." Gulliver couldn't stop staring at his father's picture. "For me. He wanted to check on me and I, um. I needed his help with something," he finished lamely.

"He was supposed to drop in on you and Toby and come right back with a report," Tia practically growled. "He should have returned before dawn so *all* of our reliable fae with portal magic weren't *all* in the human realm ... at the *same* time." By the time she finished, her teeth were bared in a grimace and Gullie knew he really was in trouble this time.

And yet, his father had stayed. To help with Sophie. Guilt gnawed at him. His father had broken his promise to the Queen of Iskalt just to be there for his son and to make sure he was okay.

"He was supposed to go back right after he checked in with Toby." Gulliver could hardly breathe. Griff could get out of the human realm at any time during the night, but still, he was there. Because Gulliver hadn't looked out for Toby, hadn't kept him from getting involved with Xavier and his friends. And something horrible had happened.

When Brea spoke, her voice quivered. "They're calling them terrorists. I know the kinds of people humans put that label on. Why haven't they come home?" Both could open portals, and yet, neither have.

Gulliver pulled the paper closer, his eyes skimming the words. He shook his head. "This can't be right. They're saying the two men pictured are suspects of a terrorist attack on some remote village outside the city. The victims were largely families with small children." It didn't make sense. "The fae are trying to prevent more attacks, not carry them out."

"But how did they get their pictures?" Lochlan asked.

"From the crosswalks in the city," Brea said. "They can get a picture of anyone that way."

"Then how do they know they were involved in this attack?" Tia demanded, scowling her fury at Gullie.

"It's likely that someone has accused them," Brea said. "But who?"

"HAFS," Gullie said with a deep sigh, bracing himself for Tia's temper.

"Okay, why don't we back up and let Gullie tell us everything that happened before he left for Lenya." Brea had a much kinder look for him than Tia.

He explained everything about his time in New Orleans, about Toby and his new fae friends. The bombings, the attacks on fae. Tia had been right when she sent him there. It was escalating.

"If the humans capture them ..." Brea covered her mouth with her hand. "My boy."

"No." Tia leaned forward, staring at her brother's image. "If they capture him, he can escape through a portal. And

Griff has Iskalt magic along with his O'Shea portal magic. Neither should be in any real danger."

"But why haven't they contacted us?" Lochlan asked the question they were all too afraid to voice.

"Because." Eavha stopped at the end of the table, "they probably can't." Two servants set silver mugs of chilled cider in front of each of them. "No wine. I figured you all wanted clear heads tonight."

All eyes were on her now.

"What do you mean, they can't?" Tia said.

"With our crystals, a Lenyan can be as powerful as any Iskaltian, but there are limitations. We cannot draw on our magic when we're ..."

"When you're what?"

"There is so much about the portal magic still unknown to you. Maybe it has similar rules to ours."

Tia stood. "When you're what?" she repeated.

"Near death."

"No." She shook her head. "Absolutely not." She picked up the paper and shook it. "We have proof they survived the attack."

"Not necessarily, Tia," Brea said with a shaky breath. "Those pictures could have come from before the attack. But the good news is that the humans are looking for them. That means they haven't been caught yet. So wherever they are, if one or both of them are hurt, they're likely on their own."

Gulliver didn't want to think about losing anyone else he cared about, but he couldn't ignore the truth. "This group, Human Alliance For Survival, never just plans one attack. This attack is part of a greater objective. We don't know where Toby and Griff are, but if they're fighting HAFS, we need to figure out what's coming next to learn where they might go."

Everyone stared at him, no one speaking. Waiting. Two ex-sovereigns, one current one, and a duchess of Lenya thought he—Gulliver—would have the answer.

"Gullie." Tia reached out and grabbed his hand, her voice softer now. "You spent time in New Orleans around these people. Did you learn anything at all that might tell us of this objective of theirs?"

He hadn't. He still had no idea what HAFS really wanted, but he didn't think it was random chaos or just killing a few fae. Yet, he knew someone who might.

He closed his eyes for a moment, drawing in a deep breath. This wasn't why he'd brought Sophie here. She wasn't a prisoner forced to give up information.

Still, Toby and Griff were on the line.

"I wasn't there long enough." The tension in the room deflated, a balloon of hope losing its air. "But there is someone here who might help us."

Chapter Two
SOPHIE-ANN

"This isn't happening." Sophie rushed into the room that now felt like her only haven in a sea of strange and foreign things. "It's not real." That power. The way Gulliver skidded across the courtyard and couldn't stop himself.

Her dad was right.

Magic had no place in any world, not if it took free will so completely. It was an abomination. Slamming the heavy door shut, she searched the room for anything she could use to barricade it. The tea table would have to do.

She gripped the edge of the heavy, black furniture that seemed to spark and come alive. A strange vibration ran the length of her arms, but she had to have imagined it. It took all her strength—a strength she hadn't had in years—to pull the table across the room to the door. She cleared off the silver tray on top of it and braced it beneath the door handle.

Backing away from the door, she put her hands on her

hips and drew in a breath. Her heart thrummed against her breastbone, the pulse pounding in her ears.

That woman out there terrified her. She'd used her power so casually, as if there was nothing wrong with forcing it on Gulliver. Was that what they all did? She could still hear that voice echoing against the stones. *Don't get mad?* She didn't understand anything that was said, but it was clear Gulliver knew who she was and that he had angered the powerful fae woman.

Sophie fumbled back farther into her room and managed to sit on the edge of the bed before her legs collapsed beneath her. She wanted to scream, or throw up, or run away into the wilderness of this awful world.

But, no. That wasn't what she wanted at all. "I want to go home." She flopped onto her back, staring at the pearl gray canopy above her head. There was luxury here of a kind she wasn't used to, but she'd give it all away to curl up in her own bed.

Thoughts of home calmed her mind enough for her to truly consider her situation. She was a prisoner in the fae world, the same fae who turned most of the human world dark for months. If they could do that, could take her mother from her, what else were they capable of?

If only her father could have seen her today playing a strange game with those he despised. He'd have been ashamed of her. But would he have also been grateful they saved her life? There was the problem. She couldn't remember the last time she felt this good, and it was because they saved her with their magic.

Did that erase everything else they'd done? The danger they posed to her entire world? Or was the fact that Gulliver had to force his way into the healing pools just another sign of their corruption? That they had healing pools capable of bringing her back from the brink of death, yet they didn't allow free use of such magic when untold lives—human or fae—could be saved from illnesses like hers.

A soft knock sounded on the door, and she sat so fast her head swam. Clamping her lips shut, she didn't say a word.

They knocked again. And waited.

Sophie's gaze darted around the room, searching for anything she could use as a weapon. Her eyes fell on the fireplace and the tools sitting next to it. She climbed off the bed and tiptoed across the room, wrapping her fingers around the cool iron poker.

Her father said fae couldn't touch iron. It burned them like the demons he believed them to be.

"I know you're in there," an irritated voice said as the woman jiggled the doorknob. "You do realize I can open this door no matter what you've done to it, right? I'd rather you not have to see that, but I am coming in. It's your choice how."

Sophie couldn't find the words to respond, so she readied herself, planting her feet as far apart as the obnoxious dress she'd been given would let her. She lifted the poker, prepared to attack.

A sigh came through the door. "Guess we're doing this the hard way." The tray slipped from underneath the knob and shot across the room. The table moved, seemingly of its own accord, scraping across the floor until the door was clear.

When it finally opened, a small woman stood there, arms crossed and eyebrows raised. "Well, I can see why Gullie likes you." She stepped into the room. "Give me the poker. I'm really not in the mood to fight with a human."

Sophie stepped back, shaking her head. "Stay away from me."

The woman rubbed her eyes. "I am way too tired for this.

Do you know what I've been through lately because of your father?"

"No more than you deserve."

"Come now, I know you don't believe that. Gullie wouldn't be so ... attached if you did."

Sophie narrowed her eyes. "He can keep his attachment to himself." She wasn't sure if she meant it. The Gulliver she met at the Vieux Carré Cafe was still lodged deep in her heart. He'd cared for her, and she'd thought he was the kindest man she'd ever met.

The woman reached out, and the poker slid from Sophie's fingers, dropping to the floor with a loud clang. "I might have let you keep that so you'd at least have the illusion of protecting yourself, but then you had to go and insult Gulliver. You'll learn quickly that's the best way to get on my bad side."

"Do you have a good side? You're fae." The words sounded too much like her father's, and she wasn't sure she liked it.

The woman's shoulders dropped. "This is going to be harder than I thought. Look, I'm trying really hard not to go all angry, scary, magical queen on you right now."

She sounded so human. "Y-you're a queen?"

A smile curved her lips. "Queen Tierney of Iskalt, at your service. You can call me Tia because, honestly, my parents were daft naming me Tierney after the grandmother I never met. It's such a stuffy old name, and I am fun."

She said it with a growl in her voice, and Sophie shrank away. "You sound fun."

A surprised laugh popped out of Tia. "I think I'm going to like you once you stop acting so freaking terrified of me. I'm really not so scary. Sure, I'm more powerful than just about any other fae, but I mostly use my magic to play pranks on Gullie and my siblings. Sometimes, I break out of dungeons or destroy ancient magical barriers, but only when I'm really looking for a good time."

This woman was insane. Sophie knew it without a doubt. From the casual way she spoke of magic to the feats she claimed.

"I can tell you don't believe me. Was it the pranks? Do you think queens don't get to have some fun?" She shook her head. "Look, what you believe or don't isn't my problem. I have bigger friends to fry."

"Fish," Sophie whispered, not sure why she felt the need to correct her.

Tia winked. "Oh, I know. I prefer my way, mostly when I'm talking to Gulliver after he has brought a human into the fae realm to use some of our most protected magic. You're lucky I wasn't here when he arrived. I'd have let you die."

"Thanks?"

"Don't take it personally. Humans really aren't my problem. Not unless they're hunting down my brother and my uncle for crimes I know they couldn't have committed."

Sophie didn't know what she was talking about.

Tia continued. "Look, I don't want us to be enemies, but I've never really cared how many of those I make. Just ask my husband. He was my enemy once upon a time, and then he realized I was always right. But you owe me."

"How do you figure that?" Sophie was waiting for the queen to use her magic to get information, was prepared for the pain to come. Yet, it didn't.

"My uncle Griff brought you here. He saved your life."

Sophie shook her head. "Gulliver—"

"Can't open portals. His father helped him, and now, that

father is in danger because of some idea that he can save my harebrained brother. They've attached themselves to a group of fae in the human realm, and the newspaper claims they are terrorists."

Guilt gnawed at Sophie. If it was true that this man saved her, did she have an obligation to him?

Tia pointed to the settee. "Sit. We have much to discuss and only so much time before Gulliver runs into this room to make sure I'm not roasting you over the fire."

"You would do that?" she breathed.

A smile parted the fae queen's lips. "Man, you humans. You really do believe we're awful. Well, we're not the ones currently attacking our own people to seek out those different from us. I suggest you sit and tell me everything you know, or I might have to revise the whole roasting over the fire bit."

This time, Sophie knew she was joking. It seemed the woman did that a lot but didn't want others to know when something was a joke. Sophie did as told, lowering herself to the settee in front of the cold embers, thankful there was no fire at the moment. It meant there'd be no roasting.

Tia didn't sit, instead she paced in front of the settee. "Your father is the leader of this anti-fae group, is he not?"

Sophie nodded. "Well ... one of them, at least. But Just in New Orleans."

"The attacks are escalating. We've tracked his activities for a while. It's why I sent Gulliver to New Orleans. He was meant to gather intel from local fae." She rubbed the back of her neck and stopped walking. "I should have acted earlier, should have sent more than my friend and my brother into the human city, but we do not want a war with the humans."

"Is that why you turned our entire world dark?" Sophie looked up at her, defiance burning in her eyes. "That wasn't war?"

Tia's brow furrowed. "That was over ten years ago, and we didn't—"

"Ten years or not, some of us never got to move on." Like her mother. Like her family.

"Is that what this is about? An accident that we did everything we could to fix?"

Sophie didn't believe for one second it was an accident. How does one accidentally block the sun from shining?

Tia dropped to the settee beside her. "We were at war, human. Yes, an evil fae king ripped open the world and let darkness seep into yours, but we defeated him. My brother, who your people currently call a terrorist, helped me return order and good to both our worlds. And now, he bears the blame for acts your father commits. How is that justice?"

"Justice?" Sophie jumped to her feet. "Do not speak to me of justice." If that truly existed, her mother would still be alive.

Tia was quiet for a long moment. "We've lost those we care about too."

It wasn't just someone she cared about; it was her mother. "It's not the same thing."

"Of course it is. You think we're so different, but you're wrong. My mother grew up in the human realm, and I've spent a lot of time there. Our main differences are only perception. As the existence of fae and magic comes into the open, it's natural for you to fear us. But we have families too. We laugh and love and play with our children. There is good and bad in both our worlds, but all we can do is fight so that the good wins out in the end. I wish that meant we could prevent evil, but that's impossible."

Sophie turned away, not wanting Tia to see the tears burning in her eyes. Most of her life, she'd been so angry because she thought her mother's death had been preventable. That the very existence of the fae caused that tragedy.

But when Tia continued, she heard every word. "Last year, I stood on the gallows of this very castle with Gulliver at my side and a noose around my neck."

Slowly rotating back around, Sophie met her gaze, her heart plummeting at the thought of Gulliver facing his own demise. He must have been so scared.

Tia nodded. "It was bad. My husband saved us, but I will never forget how it felt to stand in the face of evil and lose. Weeks later, my brother lost the love of his life as we fought to save those very fae who'd tried to kill me so many times."

"How did you do it? How did you forgive them?" Sophie blurted, half wishing she could call the questions back.

She drew in a deep breath. "I realized there was nothing to forgive. Most of the fae in Lenya had nothing to do with my almost execution. They just wanted to live their lives and hope to avoid the noose themselves. The man who'd sentenced me was already dead, and that was good enough for me. I couldn't punish an entire kingdom just because something bad happened to me."

For so long, Sophie only focused on herself. Such was the nature of a disease like hers. Every day, every moment, her inner focus was on how she was feeling. Could she take her shift at the cafe? Did she feel capable of getting out of bed? It could make a person imagine they are the only suffering one.

But Tia suffered too. She saw it in the queen's eyes, heard it in her voice.

Even with that bit of understanding, the anger didn't subside. She once again pictured Gulliver as the magic pulled him through the gates. No matter the intentions of those wielding such power, it was too dangerous to be allowed to exist.

The fae might be similar to humans in some ways, but if they chose, they could destroy her world. Her father was wrong about a lot of things, but at least he knew the only way to survive was to strike first, to never back down.

If they did, all was lost.

Chapter Three
TOBY

"Watch it, Xavier." Toby winced as his half-fae friend removed the bandage from his shoulder.

"Then, sit still and it might not hurt so much." Xavier examined the open wound on Toby's shoulder. During the last skirmish with the humans, Toby was shot, and he was still recovering. The bullet had hit him straight on but passed clean through muscle and tissue just below the joint. He was lucky, but the injury let him with a wound that had bled a lot. He'd thought he was dying at the time. He'd even thought Logan had come for him, but the person he saw just before he passed out was his uncle. It seemed Griffin had arrived not long after the fighting began in the small village.

Xavier dabbed a potion over Toby's injury, and the sting set his whole arm on fire.

"I'm sorry, all we have to clean injuries is alcohol." He frowned at the state of the wound. "It will only sting for a minute, and then it'll subside."

"Hot water works too," Toby muttered.

Xavier chuckled. "Not enough to kill germs." He rummaged around his potions kit and smoothed a layer of salve over the stitches the local healer had given him. It didn't seem to work as well as fae potions did. Toby had a throbbing headache and his whole arm ached from shoulder to wrist.

"What are germs, and why do they need killing?"

"They're what are making this injury swell up and throb." Xavier looked worried about the wound, but Toby felt fine except for the terrible headache that plagued him.

"That looks awful." Griffin peered over Xavier's shoulder. "When I take you home, you're going straight to the palace healers." Griffin tapped his foot impatiently against the rough wooden floor of the barn where they were currently hiding out. With their faces splattered all over the news and in the human papers, Griffin and Toby were stuck, and the village elders wouldn't let them use their portal magic within the town limits. It was too dangerous to use magic when HAFS members were scattered across the city and surrounding areas in droves, just looking for anything that resembled magic.

"I've told you, Uncle Griff, I'm not going back." Toby sucked in a breath as Xavier re-wrapped the bandages tightly around his shoulder. "I know you've come to check up on me, but you should go home and give my sister an update. "Ouch! Take it easy Xavier." He winced

"Sorry." Xavier eased up on the pressure against the wound. "You have to promise me you'll keep ice on this. It will help with the swelling."

"That's such a weird thing. It can't possibly be true. I come from a land of ice, and I can promise you it's not good for much."

"Just do it, Toby." Xavier stood, forcing Toby to lie back against the cot.

He was sick of resting. Resting meant there was far too much time to think about things he didn't want to think about. He preferred action. Fighting the humans gave him a purpose, and he wanted to protect the fae living in a world that would never accept them. He knew something about being different from everyone around him. Luckily for him, his people had never hated him for his lack of magic.

"Fine. I'll ice it, but I'm not staying cooped up in this smelly old barn for another minute." He tried to sit, but Griffin pushed him back down.

"Your mother would have my head if I let you out of that bed before you're completely healed."

"I'm fine, Griff. Just a headache is all." Toby compromised by sitting on the edge of the cot. He and Griffin were the only ones staying in the barn at the moment, but there were several other cots laid out in rows across the hayloft. The fae community was a small one made up of a few farms and a central town square. The barn stood near the square and served as a meeting hall and winter storage when it wasn't being used as a hospital.

"I'll come back to check on you later," Xavier said. "If the swelling doesn't go down by then, I'll send for the healer again. You might need a shot of penicillin."

"I've been shot once already. I don't want to go through that again any time soon."

Xavier chuckled, shaking his head, probably at something Toby said that sounded funny to him. He did that a lot, but Xavier seemed to enjoy it. "Get some rest." Xavier scaled the ladder to the lower part of the barn.

"He's right, you know." Griffin sat on the cot opposite

Toby's. "You need to rest. I don't think you've slept much since we got here."

"I don't sleep well most nights." Toby watched through the huge hayloft window as Xavier made his way down the wellworn path to the town square. With a sigh he rubbed a weary hand across his face. He hadn't slept well since Logan died. When he did sleep, he woke from horrible dreams where he relived the moment of his death over and over. Staying awake or drunk was easier than facing his dreams.

"I could open a portal right now, and we would be gone before anyone even knew what happened."

"And what if someone saw us?" He shook his head stubbornly. "It's too risky when these people don't know who they can trust. There could be HAFS members right here among them, and these fae wouldn't know since half of them don't have strong fae features. It's hard fighting against something you can't really see."

"I am very familiar with such things." Griffin's voice dropped into a sympathetic tone. The kind of tone fae had adopted around him after he'd lost Logan. It made him so angry to hear the pity and sorrow others would never understand.

"I need to stay and fight, Uncle Griff." Toby stood and crossed the loft to the big window overlooking the small village on the outskirts of New Orleans. The countryside was beautiful here. It reminded him of Fargelsi along the marshlands, but even more beautiful and less scary than what the Southern Vatlands used to be.

"Is it this Xavier fellow?" Griffin asked carefully. "Is he someone ... special to you?"

"No." Toby's voice came out in an angry rush. "It's not about that."

"Then, tell me what it is about. Every time I mention

going home, you get defensive and refuse to leave."

"I can't leave when there are fae who need help. These people live with very little magic. Most of them are half-human and half-fae like Xavier. Their magic is weak if they have it at all. The ones they believe are powerful pale in comparison to even the weakest of fae in the five kingdoms."

"I see." Griffin looked down at his hands. "They are more like you."

"Yes. And I won't leave them when I know something about fighting against a formidable foe without the benefit of magic."

"Prince Tobias, the Ogre Killer," Griffin said softly. "It's ... admirable, and I can understand your reasons for wanting to stay, but our faces are everywhere. It isn't safe."

"I don't care about that. I can protect myself."

"I know you can. You've been trained to fight. You understand strategy and warfare, but no matter what you feel, this isn't your fight. You've learned the hard way that humans have weapons we do not understand."

"I know now." Toby ran a hand over his fresh bandage. "And I will be more careful, but I won't leave, Uncle Griff. But I think you should find a quiet place, late at night, and slip back home to tell Tia what's happening here."

"Your sister will just come here looking for you."

"Don't let her." Toby smirked. "You control portals, and we all know she can't."

"And you know very well that would be like trying to hold the waves back from the shore. If she thinks you're in danger, she'll try portaling here herself if she has to."

Toby looked up into the familiar eyes of his birth father, begging him to understand. "When you lived in Gelsi, back when Queen Reagan was at her most powerful, you lived alone in your cottage away from palace life."

Griffin nodded. "It was easier for me there."

"Because you were an Iskaltian prince who couldn't go home to Iskalt?"

"Yes. And no." He hung his head. "I look back on that time now, and I believe I preferred living at the cottage so I didn't have to see the Fargelsian people suffer under her rule. I loved her. She was my mother, and for a long time, I refused to see her as she was."

"You felt for the people of Gelsi?"

"I did. I was ashamed of my inability to help them." Griffin studied Toby's face. "You feel for these fae here in the human world?"

"I do." Toby nodded, dragging in a deep breath. "And it's been a very long time since I've felt anything."

"Uncle Griff, wake up." Toby shook his uncle, just short of rolling him off the cot he'd slept on for the three nights they'd spent in the fae village. "It's time for you to leave."

"Leave?" Griffin groaned, his bones creaking and popping as he stretched. "Where am I going?" He sat on the edge of the cot, rubbing the sleep from his eyes.

"I need you to go home," Toby said simply. "There's been an attack on another fae village farther to the south of New Orleans. This isn't going to stop." He studied his uncle's eyes. "We've seen this all before, Griff. We know what it leads to, and we can't let that happen here."

Griffin nodded. "It will be far worse here with the humans and their killing machines." He reached for his pack. "Are you sure I can't talk you into coming with me?"

"No. I need you to tell Tia everything that's happening

here. I'm not so certain the fae in the human world can protect themselves from HAFS much longer." He moved to the window to peer out into the darkness where fae were gathering to discuss the latest news.

"I brought you one of her spelled journals; you can tell her yourself." Griffin moved to stuff his feet into his boots.

"I won't use it." Toby shoved his few belongings into a pack. "Once I open that book, Tia won't shut up, and I can't have her tie my hands while I'm trying to help these people save their little corner of this world. I need you to be the messenger."

"And what am I to tell your sister, the queen, when she asks why you refused the journal?"

"I don't care. Make something up." He shrugged. "Better yet, tell her I'm trying to do what she sent me here to do."

Griffin quickly gathered the last of his things. "Where am I going to open a portal where no one will see me?"

"Xavier will be here in a moment to take you deep into the bayou where it should be safe and no one will see the light. You'll portal home just before dawn."

"Very well. What do you propose your sister do to aid you in this fight against HAFS?"

"To start, we need more trained soldiers. Not an army, but advisors to help the fae here protect the innocents. These minor attacks are just the beginning. This unrest is about to burst wide open, and the fae are going to need representatives to act in their best interests."

"You act as if a war is brewing."

Toby lifted his pack over his shoulder. "That's exactly what I'm saying, Griff. War is coming to the human realm, and we need to be ready for it."

Chapter Four
GULLIVER

"Tell me again how the humans got their pictures in the first place?" Tia paced across the large sitting room in the royal residence where Eavha and Declan now lived. "It looks like they're being followed." She snatched the newspaper from Gullie's hands as he stalked past her in the opposite direction. "Just look at them!" She threw her arms up in the air. "They look like ... like they're up to something ... like ..."

"Terrorists? No." Gulliver ran a hand through his hair as he hit the end of the sitting room and turned around, pacing back across the plush navy blue carpet. It glittered with tiny specks of crystals, making the floor look like the midnight sky. Eavha had done a lot of redecorating since he'd last visited the Vondurian palace. "They look like two fae trying to blend in with the humans around them and neither one of them is very good at it. They're just crossing the street, probably trying to figure out how the trolly cars work, but in the paper, along with the article about how fae are attacking humans, they look guilty."

"But how did a street corner manage to get a picture of them?"

"It's from something called a traffic camera, Tia." Gulliver's tail swished behind him as he passed her again. "It works on its own, but I don't really know how. It does seem like they're being followed, though. Maybe there's more to it than a traffic camera?"

"Like what, Gullie?" she snapped, magic crackling at her fingertips, making Sophie flinch from her seat on one of the many settees scattered across the room. "What is happening to my fae in the human world?"

"Keep your hair on already. We already knew people of HAFS were attacking the fae communities, and they don't care if humans get hurt too. They're getting bold now, trying to blame their terrorism on the fae. That's really all I can tell you. Griff and Toby were just in the wrong place at the wrong time. Easy scapegoats to pin the attacks on."

"These people sound like lunatics."

Gulliver winced, averting his eyes from Sophie's. "None of that matters. We just need to get in there, find those two idiots, and bring them home."

"But where are they?" Tia marched back across the room, biting her fingernails—a nervous habit from her childhood she'd never quite kicked.

"The paper says they're wanted, which means they haven't been arrested yet." Gulliver had watched enough local news on the feletision box that was stuck on the news channel during their stay at the Lamothe House Inn. There were always criminals wanted for some crime or another in the city.

"Which means they're hiding somewhere, likely injured

or unable to use their portal magic, and we have to find them before the human authorities do." Tia balled her hands into fists at her sides. "I don't want to even think about the nightmare of them getting arrested and then disappearing from their jail cells through magic portals the humans won't understand. We cannot afford to cause any more magical commotion or we really are going to have a confrontation with the humans."

"Exactly." Gulliver whirled around, his tail nearly knocking over a priceless Vondurian vase perched on a marble pedestal. He leaped to catch it and set it back carefully before he continued his movements. "They're probably hiding out with Xavier somewhere in the city."

"Who is this Xavier, and can we trust him?"

"He's a friend of Sophie's. That's why I asked her to meet with us." He turned to Sophie where she sat wide eyed and silent on the settee. "Where would Xavier hide any friends who were trying to avoid your father?"

"I don't know. He wouldn't tell me." She held a fluffy, cream-colored pillow in her lap like a shield that would protect her from Tia's magic.

"Would you know how to find this friend of yours?" Tia demanded, striding across the room toward the girl. "Could you get a message to him?"

Sophie let out a startled squeak as Tia approached her.

"Tia, take it down a notch." Gulliver put himself between the two women. "She's not your subject, and she's scared."

"I'm not scared." Sophie lifted her chin in defiance. "I'm furious I've been brought here against my will."

"You honestly would have rather died than let Gulliver save your life in the healing pools?" Tia turned on Gulliver. "Which I have not forgotten about, by the way. We're going to have to talk about your punishment when all this is over. King

Hector is furious with you, and Bron is itching to get her hands on you. You broke about a dozen new laws when you took it upon yourself to heal this girl. You might be my most favorite person in all the worlds, but even I can't save you this time."

"Focus, Tia. We can talk about that later. Right now, we need to save my dad and your brother."

"Griff was my uncle before he was your dad." Tia crossed her arms over her chest.

"You people are so strange," Sophie muttered, glancing between the two old friends.

Gulliver's tail twitched furiously as he pointed at her. "You didn't even know he existed when Dad found me in the slums of the Myrkur palace."

"I knew him from my dreams." She stood with her hands on her hips. "Besides, Uncle Griff likes me better than you." She returned to her pacing. "Sophie, what about getting that message to your friend in the city? Is it possible?"

"Maybe. I don't really know." Sophie shrank back from Tia's intensity.

"We need to find out what's happened to our family, Sophie," Gulliver said, approaching her like he would a startled deer. "This is my dad and Tia's brother we're talking about. I know you're overwhelmed with everything that's happened these last few days." He sank down onto the chair closest to her without invading her space. "But neither Griff nor Toby would ever hurt anyone. I promise you, they are good fae. We have to get them out of there before they suffer the punishment for someone else's crimes." He left it unsaid that some of those crimes were committed by her own father.

Sophie nodded. "If you let me go home, I'll do whatever I can to find Xavier, and then he can help you find your family if he wants to. I want nothing more to do with any of this."

She sniffed back her tears and put on a brave face. "I am grateful for whatever you've done to heal me, but I-I can't be involved with this ... unrest between the fae and the humans."

"Well, from what I hear, you and your family are already involved." Tia glared at Sophie, looking every inch the scary ice queen.

Sophie shook her head. "My father isn't a bad man."

"So, he's the good kind of man who kills innocent fae children and humans who happen to get in the way?"

"Tia, that's enough." Lochlan strode into the room with Brea right behind him. "We could hear you two bickering all the way down the hall. You'll wake the whole palace with all your shouting."

"Sorry, Dad." Tia waved a hand at him.

"Well, I had hoped you two would come to an agreement for once in your lives, but as much as I don't care to admit it, my brother can take care of himself."

"And so can Toby," Brea added. "They will do whatever it takes to stay hidden until the dust settles. If they get into too much trouble, they can portal home whenever they want. That they haven't just tells us they are still trying to help the fae who might not be as capable."

"What are you saying, Mom? That we should just let them fend for themselves?" Tia demanded.

"That's exactly what she is saying," Lochlan said.

"But what if Eavha was right and they can't portal home because they're hurt, or dying?"

"We can't think like that, sweetheart." Brea crossed the room to pull her daughter into her embrace. "There is a lot more at stake here than Griff and Toby ending up on the FBI's Most Wanted list."

"What's the FBI?" Tia muttered into her mother's shoulder.

"Nothing to worry about right now. We need to focus our efforts on ending this unrest between the fae and this HAFS group before it gets out of hand."

"It's already out of hand," Sophie said, seeming surprised that she'd spoken her thoughts out loud.

Brea moved to sit opposite Sophie. "I grew up in the human realm, Sophie. I know firsthand how scary it is to wake up one day and find yourself in a world of magic you never knew existed. And having a bunch of scary fae demanding your cooperation. I am so sorry you've ended up here in the middle of all this, but I promise we will get you home just as soon as we can."

"But you're fae." Sophie stared at the former queen's pointed ears.

"I didn't know that until I was almost eighteen. At heart, I'm a human girl who grew up on a farm in Ohio. And I care about all the people—fae and human—that could die so needlessly, simply because they do not understand each other. We need to know what the HAFS group is planning so we can try to end the violence. If you could help us find my son and his uncle, I would be forever grateful."

"You don't understand." Sophie sucked in a shaky breath. "The fae killed my mother. My father will never trust anyone who has magic. Even if they did heal me. He'll see it as some form of manipulation to get close to him and HAFS." Her whole body trembled, and Gulliver wanted to comfort her. "I won't betray him. I-I'm sorry. I can't help you." She shot up from her seat, still clutching the pillow to her chest. "Especially not when you continue to keep me here against my will. All I've heard since I woke are promises that I will get to go home soon. So far, that seems to be the very last thing any of you intend to do. Yet, you expect me to betray my people to help you."

"We healed you!" Tia's eyes flashed with magic. "The least you could do is help us save our family."

"With all due respect, your Majesty," Sophie spat. "You didn't heal me. Gulliver did. And he used the healing pools of this kingdom to do it. Correct me if I am wrong, but you are not the sovereign here. I don't owe you anything." She dropped the pillow to the floor, clutching the skirt of her gown in her fists. Her chest heaved with fury.

Secretly, Gulliver was proud to see the sweet, mild-tempered girl stand up for herself.

"So, how's everyone's week going?" A familiar teasing voice broke the tension in the room.

"Dad!" Gulliver whirled around to gape at his father leaning against the entrance to the sitting room. "You're okay?" He darted across the room and flung his arms around his father. "Are you hurt? You look awful." He studied the bruises on his face and the cracked knuckles of his hands. The dark circles under his eyes.

"Griffin, you look like you've been in a fight." Brea ushered him to a nearby seat.

"A fight with a human bomb sending a poor defenseless fae village into unnecessary chaos." He sank into the chair, looking more exhausted than Gulliver had ever seen him. "The unrest there is growing by the day."

"Where is Toby?" Tia asked as she and Lochlan crowded around him.

All the color drained from Griffin's face as he turned toward Brea. "He's okay, but he's been shot."

"Shot!" Brea clapped a hand over her mouth.

"He's fine. Or he will be with a little more rest. It hit him in the shoulder, but the human-fae healer said it was a clean shot. Toby's in a lot of pain from the swelling, but he has people caring for him."

"It's infected? Has he seen a doctor? No, of course he hasn't because you and my son are wanted terrorists." She punched his arm and appeared on the cusp of a tirade Gulliver usually only saw from Tia. A talent she got from her mother.

"Brea, that son of yours got himself into trouble without my help." Griffin threw up his hands to block any further punches. "He's working with the fae to fight HAFS and stop the hate crimes. He's determined to end the struggle between fae and humans. You'd be proud of him."

"How did you know we were in Lenya?" Brea's anger wilted for a moment.

"I didn't. I came to check on my son first." He glanced apologetically at Gulliver.

"You intended to wait two more days before you brought this news to me?" Brea's eyes flashed gold with the intensity of her Eldurian magic.

"No, that's not what I intended at all." Griffin held a hand out to stall her yelling. "I was going to send you a message."

"Wait, you gave Toby the spelled journal, didn't you, Uncle Griff?" Tia said, excitement making her eyes seem larger than normal. "I forgot all about it. I have mine in my rooms. We can write to him and make a plan!" She turned to leave.

"He wouldn't take it." Griffin reached for his bag. "I was going to use it to send you a message about Toby once I had a chance to check in on Gullie and his friend." He turned to Sophie, where she still stood frozen with uncertainty. "I am glad to see you are still with us, Sophie." He gave her a polite nod. "And I must say you look much healthier than the last time I saw you."

"Th-thank you," she muttered, some of the tension wilting from her shoulders.

"Now that we're all here and we know Toby is safe for the moment," Lochlan interjected, "I think it's time we all return to Iskalt and discuss our next steps with our peers across the five kingdoms. It's the most central location, and Neeve and Myles are already there with King Hector. The council of royals will need a say in whatever is to happen next. In the meantime, perhaps we can get a message to Sophie's friend Xavier if she is willing." He turned toward Sophie. "No one will force you to do anything you don't want to do, but we would appreciate it if you could help us find our son. Either way, I will take you home myself as soon as we've explained your situation to the other rulers of this land. They will need to know of your healing at the very least. You have my word."

Sophie stared at the formidable Lochlan O'Shea for a long moment before she gave one solitary nod.

Chapter Five
SOPHIE-ANN

Nothing here made any sense. One moment, the man they called Griffin was a wanted terrorist in the human realm, and the next, he stood before his family in Lenya, speaking to her as if they'd met.

What kind of person showed up in the middle of the night like it was no big deal? Sophie yawned, trying to shake off her need for sleep. Things were happening and she needed to pay attention. She just wondered if these fae ever slept.

Over the years, one of the greatest mysteries HAFS tried to uncover was how exactly the fae got to their world. Now, she was so close to learning their deepest secret. If only she could get a message to her father and explain everything she'd learned. Maybe it would help him bring an end to this decade-long struggle.

Sophie shrank in on herself under the curious gaze of the handsome newcomer. He spoke as if they were old friends. Surely she'd remember such an encounter?

Gulliver walked across the room with a purpose, and she turned so she didn't have to look at him, didn't have to meet his startling eyes with Tia's words still rattling in her mind. Forgiveness had never been a Deveraux strength, and she wasn't there yet. If she ever would be.

Steps echoed off the high ceilings of the hall as Gulliver joined his father. "I sent Mom a message with Loch." He sighed. "She's going to be so angry with you."

Griffin's lips split into a smile. "You mean she'll be vexed I didn't invite her along."

"Probably both. The message won't reach her before Hector tells her of the summons to the Iskalt palace, but at least this way, we can say we sent it."

"Good man." Griffin draped an arm over his son's shoulders. It looked so natural, so ... human. Sophie stole glances their way as the two of them continued to chat like the world wasn't on the brink of disaster.

Tia clapped her hands. "Okay, my parents have left for Iskalt and to gather the other royals for an emergency meeting. Eavha will stay here and keep Lenya running in the queen's absence. Now, the four of us need to go. Dawn will be upon us soon."

What did dawn have to do with anything? There was so much Sophie didn't know, and she was torn between wanting to absorb everything for some later advantage and just wanting to find her bed for whatever remained of the night.

"Uncle." Queen Tierney nodded to Griffin. "If you will."

They brought no supplies for a long journey, had packed few belongings, and yet, no one appeared to notice.

Eavha stood in the doorway, a sad smile on her face. "Be careful, Tia."

Tia didn't respond because at that moment the atmosphere grew thick, distorting the view of the opposite end of the room. Sophie scrambled back as the power trailed down her arms. That was when she saw his eyes.

Griffin's normally green eyes shone violet as he concentrated on the air before him that began to swirl and take on the same hue. It was light at first, mesmerizing. For a moment, Sophie forgot to be scared. For a moment, she wanted a closer look.

That moment snapped as his magic expanded and a blast of wind blew the hair away from her face.

"Go!" Griffin yelled.

Without hesitation, Tia disappeared into the violet tunnel. A scream lodged in Sophie's throat, but it didn't make it past her lips. She couldn't move, not until she felt Gulliver's hand in hers.

He tugged her close, wrapping an arm tightly around her. "There's no time to be human right now." He yanked her hard, and together they fell. The drop seemed to go on forever. There was nothing to hold on to except Gulliver. No point to focus on in the horizon. Every part of her body propelled her forward at a nauseating pace, and when she resisted the pull of magic, pain seared through her like her limbs might rip from her body. But Gulliver's embrace kept her from spinning out of control.

She cried out, but there was no sound. This was it, the end. Was this how her mother died? Was this what it felt like to be killed by fae magic?

Color receded from her vision until all she saw was bright green grass barreling toward her at the speed of a New Orleans tram. At the last moment, Gulliver twisted himself toward the ground, and they hit hard, the impact rattling every bone in her body.

The only sound that escaped her was a long groan. She lay sprawled across Gulliver's chest, unable to move.

Someone coughed. "Not one of your best landings, Dad."

Gulliver rolled Sophie onto her side, giving her some distance between them. With another groan, he spit out a mouthful of grass.

Sophie flopped onto her back and grass prickled her skin, the ground beneath her softer than she'd expected. Gulping in a breath, she studied the sky overhead, unable to wrap her mind around what just happened.

Griff picked himself up off the ground as if he hadn't just collided with it, brushing off his pants. "It would have been easier if someone wasn't fighting the portal the entire way." He started walking away. "I need some human food."

Human food? Sophie lifted her head, taking in her surroundings. They'd landed on the lawn in front of a small farmhouse that looked like it had seen better days. A rickety porch held no furniture, only a welcome mat that said, 'leave your packages at the door, we're probably not wearing pants'.

Across the yard, the barn didn't look fit to house a pig, let alone a horse.

Tia sat up. "Well, it's a good thing my mom had the lawn reseeded."

Gulliver cracked a smile, turning it on Sophie. "We land here a lot. The ground used to be a lot harder if you can imagine that."

"Mom loves doing projects in the human realm now that she's not ruling a kingdom anymore." Tia rolled her eyes. "You can take the fae out of the human world, but you can't, well, you know ..."

How many fae grew up here without even knowing their true origins? If one with royal blood remained hidden for so long, how did HAFS stand a chance of rooting out all the others?

Before standing, Sophie took a moment to breathe in the fresh air, the air of her world. She was home. It might not be New Orleans, but wherever this farmstead was located, it was a lot closer to her beloved city than any part of the fae world.

"Ohio," Gulliver said as they walked toward the house. "That's where we are."

Tia held the door open for them. "And no, you can't run from us here. So don't get any ideas."

"Tia," Gulliver growled her name. "Enough with the threats. She's not a prisoner."

"No, but she's not quite free to go just yet." Tia gave Sophie a long stare before she entered the house.

In the kitchen, Griffin dug through cabinets, curses falling from his lips. He looked worse than he had when he first arrived at the palace in Lenya. The circles under his eyes were darker and he looked haggard.

"Something wrong, Griff?" Tia asked.

He muttered something unintelligible and kept searching. "It has to be here somewhere. I know there was at least one box left."

"A box of what?" Alarm entered Gulliver's voice. "Dad, tell me ... is it ..."

Sophie wasn't sure if she should be worried, or why the two men looked so scared. She gripped the counter, still trying to recover from that dizzying magic she had so many questions about.

"It's gone." Griffin slammed a cabinet. "I'm going to have some words for your mother, Tia."

Tears welled in Gulliver's eyes, and he blinked them away. Sophie took in the angry Griff, the upset Gulliver, and the smirking Tia, confusion clouding her mind.

"What are we going to do?" Gulliver plopped himself

down on a stool at the counter and buried his head in his hands.

"It'll be okay, son." Griff put a hand on his shoulder. "I promise we'll get through this."

Sophie couldn't handle this anymore. "Does someone want to tell me what you have to get through?"

Gulliver sniffed. "Dad ... we had ..." He shook his head, falling into silence.

"I had an entire box." Griffin looked like he wanted to rip someone's head off, and Sophie just didn't want that to be her.

"A box of what, Uncle Griff?" Tia hopped up to sit on the counter, her lips twitching.

"They were shaped like tiny square ... What do you call them?"

"Sponges, Dad." Gulliver wiped his eyes. "Adorable sponges."

"What was shaped like sponges?" It seemed as though Tia was just taunting them now.

"I don't remember what you call them."

Gulliver reached out and squeezed his father's hand. "Fruit. Sponges shaped like fruit."

They couldn't possibly ... "Are you guys talking about SpongeBob SquarePants fruit snacks?" No, that was a ridiculous thought. They couldn't possibly—

"Yes." Griffin snapped and pointed at her. "They're the best food humans have to offer."

He'd obviously never had prime rib. Or cheesecake.

Griffin wasn't done. "Last time I was here, I hid a full box in the cabinet, but it's gone. If someone is going to challenge me, it should be with a sword and shield."

Sophie shook her head, throwing her hands up as she turned. "You fae are insane." She had to get away from them.

Getting back home was paramount, but for now, she just needed some space to gather her thoughts and then she would plan her escape. Pushing through the swinging screen door, she sat on the top step, tucking the fabric of her too-long gown around her legs. The sun had started to sink on the horizon, and she tried to remember the last time she watched the sun set in her home world.

Many evenings, she'd already fallen asleep by this point, worn out by both work and treatments. She couldn't fathom a time before the illness controlled her life, dictating the wonders she got to take in.

"I'm here, Dad," she whispered, knowing the words would never reach him. She wanted him to know she was alive, that he hadn't lost her like he'd lost her mother. At least, not yet.

The door opened behind her, but she didn't turn to see who it was. The silence told her it wasn't Gulliver. Probably not Tia either.

"My son has this need ..." Griffin sat down on the step beside her, a half-eaten sandwich in his hand. "To save people. I've known him since he was two years old, and even then, he knew when someone in our village needed the kind of love he possessed. That's all he's ever wanted to do. Spread love, care for fae and humans alike. He has a big heart. Yet, he's found himself in the middle of too many wars, fighting too many battles that have all taken little pieces of his heart." He turned green eyes on hers, his no longer swirling violet with his unpredictable magic.

"Why are you telling me this?"

Taking a leisurely bite of his sandwich, he shrugged. "I know your mother died during the months of darkness, possibly by our magic, and that has to affect the way you feel about all of us."

"Possibly?" she scoffed. "A fae killed her after you turned the world dark."

His sigh echoed beside her. "Did you know one of the origins of that darkness was here in Grafton?"

She nodded. "It was the first town to go dark." She knew everything there was to learn about that time. When she didn't respond further, he continued.

"Tia's grandfather has a theory about that. Grafton, this house, is where we normally portal—at least for our generation—those few of us who have the power. He thinks we've created a thinning of the veil between worlds at each location we've entered through our magic. The more frequently we pass through the veil in one place, the weaker the veil becomes. My brother and I both used to travel here frequently when Brea was growing up. Loch more often than me. He came to watch over her. I came to spy on her. Though, that's a story for another time."

So, it was true. They were tearing her world apart.

"Why should I care about any of this?" Sophie rested her arms on her knees and leaned forward.

"Because none of it was intentional. We did not declare war on the humans, nor was your mother's death Gulliver's fault. Hate the rest of us, if you must. But Gullie is someone you can trust with your life. He's already saved it once." He stuffed the last bite of his sandwich in his mouth and some color seemed to return to his face.

Before she could respond, the door crashed open. "Found Brea's stash of chocolate." Gulliver threw his father a wrapped Milky Way. "Ready to head out?"

"Head out?" Sophie jumped to her feet. They couldn't leave yet. She was counting on having time on her side here. "Where?"

"Iskalt." Tia pushed past them to reach the lawn. "It's

why we traveled at dawn. We wanted to hit dusk here. Griffin's had some time to recover, and I've sent a message to Xavier through Mrs. Merrick, so now we can go."

"Wait who's Mrs. Merrick?" Sophie demanded.

"A friend." Tia crossed the lawn to the grassy area where they just landed.

Griffin locked the house. "All portals have to go through the human realm," he explained. "Well, all except—"

"Griff." Tia cut him off. "She is still our enemy until she decides otherwise. Watch what you tell her."

He offered her a salute, something so distinctly human it almost made Sophie laugh. Almost, because it was followed up by the air rifting once more to open that violet tunnel. The one Sophie was never setting foot in again.

She backed up. "Not happening."

"Don't be stupid." Tia grabbed her arm. "You knew you had to come back to Iskalt with us."

"But I didn't ..." She shook her head as her breath came faster and faster until it was completely out of control. "I can't." The falling. Magic coursing through her. It wasn't meant for humans, that much was clear. No one else seemed fazed at all. Didn't they see?

Gulliver pushed Tia out of the way. "It'll only last a second," he whispered. "You don't really have a choice here, Soph."

Wrong thing to say. She took off, her legs pumping as fast as she could force them.

If only she could find help, get to a human-owned house. Then, she could go home. Her lungs burned as she reached the end of the expansive lawn and circled around the back of the barn. Casting a quick glance behind her, she saw all three fae moving in.

"Tia," Gullie yelled, "don't you dare." Her eyes flicked to Tia, who'd raised a hand. "No magic."

Sophie took the momentary distraction as a chance to climb the neighbor's wooden fence, cursing whoever's idea it had been to put her in a dress. She'd almost made it over when strong hands grabbed her around the waist and yanked her back.

Kicking out, she connected with Gulliver's stomach, but he didn't release her. "Stop. Fighting. Me." He pulled her to the ground, rolling her onto her back and pinning her with his body. "I'm sorry, Sophie."

"No you aren't," she bit out.

"You have no idea what I just saved you from." He pulled away from her, yet he still didn't let her move. "Tia wouldn't have been this gentle."

"You call this gentle?" She writhed under him, trying to break his grip on her arms.

His eyes held a sadness as he shook his head. "I'm really sorry."

"For what, Gullie? Abducting me? Taking me to your world and holding me captive? Pinning me to the ground against my will."

"For that." He heaved a sigh as his brows drew together. "And for this." In one swift movement, he hauled her over his shoulder.

No amount of screaming or hammering on his back loosened his grip on her. He wasn't a muscular man, with his lean build, but he was stronger than he looked.

They reached Griffin and Tia, but before she could attempt another escape, Gulliver stepped through the portal, and her world disappeared.

Chapter Six
GULLIVER

How could Gulliver just return to Iskalt? To the rooms Tia always insisted were his, as if he were the same fae who left?

Truth: he couldn't.

Surrounded by all the opulence Iskalt provided, and all the comfort Tia demanded, he couldn't help thinking about the fae in the human world who led hidden lives. Lives that were now threatened.

This evening, Griffin left once again, not even a full day after his arrival. He went to retrieve Bron, droped her in Iskalt, and then went back to the human realm as soon as he could to check on Toby.

Now, the only fae who had any useful advice for Gulliver was gone. Useful, because Tia would try. She'd tell him what to do about Sophie, how to interact with the woman he couldn't stop thinking about. But something told him Tia's rather blunt methods would cause more harm than good.

He could still hear the fear in Sophie's screams when he

forced her through the portal. Gulliver never imagined he would ever take away a person's consent where magic was concerned. Growing up with no offensive power, he knew what it was like to feel weak in the face of so much might. And yet, he'd done that to her. Multiple times now. Taken away her choices.

He could only imagine how much she hated him for it.

Two hearths blazed in Gulliver's room, but it didn't stop the damp chill of the Iskalt palace from entering his bones. Maybe that was guilt, or maybe he was just looking for ways to punish himself.

Sitting on the four-poster feather bed, Gulliver stared at the dark blue wall opposite him. Capped with golden crown molding and dusted with the shimmer of thousands of tiny fire opals, the surface of the wall sparkled like a silver haze. Sophie was asleep on the other side of that wall, in the room where his sisters normally slept when they visited.

The wall was thin enough to hear those on the other side. He'd learned that over the years of them giggling late into the night while he tried to sleep. If he spoke right now, Sophie would have no choice but to listen to the words.

There was that word again. Choice.

He scratched his face with the tip of his tail and sighed. So much for getting some rest. Over the next few days, the royal council would arrive to meet with Tia. The last time they came together, Tia decided to send him into the human realm.

It had led them here.

None of the other rulers would be pleased Tia decided to go behind their backs for a mission they had declined to authorize. Their aim had been to remain at a distance while they watched the humans and determined if an intervention was needed. Tia had been a little more hands on than they had agreed.

Sliding from his bed, Gulliver paced the length of the room. How was he supposed to stay here and sleep when everything threatened to crash down around him? Sophie had barely left her rooms since their arrival, and he was pretty sure she would never speak to him again.

A knock at his door had him turning. It was too late for a messenger or any of the maids. There was only one person who'd wake him in the middle of the night, but when he opened the door, it wasn't Tia standing before him.

Gulliver immediately bowed, as had become his mocking habit. "Your Majesty."

Keir slapped him upside the head with the leather-bound book he carried. "Are you ever going to stop that?"

"Not on your life."

Keir sighed. "Well, are you going to let me in, or do you wish to wake the entire wing by talking in the hall?"

Gulliver held the door open wide and swept his hand out. "Please enter my humble abode, oh great Keir, ruler of nowhere, husband to a stubborn queen, annoying—"

Keir shoved the book at his chest, shutting him up. "I didn't want to wake Tia when she'd finally gotten to sleep."

"But you have no problem waking me?"

"Not really, no."

"Such a grumpy king." Gulliver rubbed his chest where the book had hit and glanced down at the leather cover, his eyes widening. "Is there a message?" This wasn't just any book. It was the journal that let the holder communicate with its twin, no matter the location.

"Do you think I came here just for the pleasure of your company?"

"In fact, most find me a joy."

"I'll just ask the human girl what she thinks of you, shall I?" Keir grunted. "Now, stop being ... you. This is serious."

Everything was serious these days. That was why Gulliver tried to make jokes, to keep everyone smiling. It was something he learned from his father. Strength came from the knowledge that one could win whatever fight they found themselves in if one could remain positive.

"Have a seat." Gulliver waved to a blue settee in front of the hearth. "I think we need a drink for this." Whatever information his father sent, it had to be important if he did it so soon after his arrival.

"Do you really think—"

"Keir." Gulliver's jaw tightened. "I'm sleeping in a room next to a girl I care about who hates everything about me. There may be a coming war between humans and fae. Foreign royals will soon learn everything Tia instructed me to do behind their back. And right here," he lifted the book, "is a piece of information that can only be bad. Let's stop with the keeping-Gulliver-sober talk for now."

Keir was quiet for a moment, and Gulliver expected an argument. He didn't have a problem with using too much alcohol, only the fact he was a terrible drunk.

"You're right." Keir shifted. "Have any Gelsi berry wine?"

"Only if you don't tell your wife I've been bringing it from Lenya every trip I make. My sister always keeps it around." It wasn't allowed in the Iskalt palace because of the dampening effect Gelsi berries had on the magic of the three kingdoms. Lucky for both Gulliver and Keir, neither of them had that kind of power.

Gulliver pulled out a bottle of the crimson gold Eavha sent him months ago. He poured two glasses and carried one to Keir. The king took it, sighing as he tilted the cup against his lips.

Taking a small sip, Gulliver set his on the low table in front of the hearth and sat in his favorite chair opposite Keir, staring at the book on the table between them.

"You're worried about him," Keir said. It wasn't a question.

"You're not? Is that not the true reason you brought this to me instead of waking Tia?" How many times had she said to both of them that sleep was for those without crowns on their heads?

Keir took a long drink, closing his eyes for that first glorious moment of pure bliss.

But Gulliver saw the battle waging inside the king. If Keir saw there was a message from Griff, he could have read it and reported to Tia, but for whatever reason, he'd known the message was for Gullie, and that probably wasn't good.

"My dad said Toby was okay last time they talked. He was in pain but not in danger." Gulliver couldn't think of Toby without feeling like he'd failed him and Tia both. She'd wanted someone to look after her grieving brother, and all Gulliver did was get distracted with a human woman while Toby involved himself in the very fight they were supposed to prevent.

"But we don't know anything about human bullets." Keir set his cup on the table and leaned forward, head in his hands. "What kind of damage do they do? His shoulder was injured. I've seen enough of those kinds of injuries to know what it means. There are no healing pools in Orleans."

"New."

"What?"

"It's New Orleans."

Keir lifted his head. "Do you think he'd be safer in Old Orleans?"

Gulliver shrugged. "New Orleans seemed pretty old to me, but if Old Orleans is older than the newer Orleans, then I guess it would have to be ancient."

"What am I going to tell my wife if we learn something has happened to her brother in New or Old Orleans?" He gestured at the book on the table between them. Both afraid to look at what news it might bring.

There was a time when Tia and Toby were almost the same fae. They did everything together. He was her anchor, her conduit. Without much magic of his own, he instead strengthened hers. A world with one and not the other was unfathomable. Tia's magic didn't work with the fire plains between them, and that had been the scariest time of her life. "Both Tia and Toby have beaten bigger odds than these."

Gulliver flipped open the notebook on the table. It was full of blank pages, but only the first page was ever used because the messages were erased once they were read. His eyes focused on his father's familiar script, barely legible, and a smile tugged at his lips.

"Can you even read that?" Keir leaned closer, trying to decipher the rough lines.

Following the words with his finger, Gulliver started reading. "Tia, your brother is fine." Both men let out long breaths. "Stubborn but alive. We have bigger problems. Every news show in the human realm has been running a story nonstop about Claude Devereaux and his missing daughter."

Gulliver let out a groan, resting his head in his hands.

"What's a news show?" Keir asked.

"I'm sure Tia has shown you a human feletision. If you hit the right buttons enough times on the black boxes, you can find shows where someone sits at a desk and tells of things happening across their world."

"That can't be real. It takes days for messages to travel."

Gulliver shook his head. As much as Tia tried to explain many of the human technologies to the Lenyan, he still failed to comprehend their technology. "Can you just believe me when I say it's important? That those news programs can reach most humans instantly?"

Keir's brows drew together, but he nodded. "Is there more?"

Gulliver searched for his place among the scribbles most wouldn't have been able to read. "The fae here are losing hope as the news claims Sophie was abducted by fae."

When Gulliver was in New Orleans, only a certain group believed in the existence of the fae. The rest thought the darkness of years ago was a phenomenon of the weather, and that HAFS members were a little loony in their beliefs. HAFS was only kept in check by other humans' limited minds. But now ...

Gulliver looked up at Keir, his father's final words echoing in his mind.

"What?"

"The humans know. Everything."

Chapter Seven
TOBY

Toby's shoulder throbbed as he flipped through the stations on the television in the tiny living room of the little house he now shared with three other fae. After the last incident with HAFS, most of the fae villagers had picked up the pieces of their lives and gone on about their business as if nothing had happened. Toby was supposed to be recovering, but he wasn't very good at resting.

Scratching at the bandages covering his wound, Toby flung the remote onto the table beside the old couch. There was nothing on, and he was slowly losing his mind.

"Sophie-Ann Devereaux is not dead." A familiar voice blasted from the television. "My daughter was abducted by the fae."

Toby leaned forward, studying the half-crazed Claude Devereaux on the screen. Bleary-eyed, with rough stubble and shadows under his eyes, the man looked as though he hadn't slept in days.

"Mr. Devereaux," the talk show host halted with a

dramatic pause, "tell us how the fae lured your daughter right from her hospital bed." The woman stared into the camera, her thick eye makeup made her seem more inhuman than the humans deemed the fae.

"My Sophie-Ann was so sick." Claude choked back a sob. "She's suffered from Leukemia since she was just a little girl, diagnosed right around the time when the world went dark." He glared at the camera, as if to say the diagnosis at that time wasn't just a coincidence.

Xavier came in, letting the back door bang shut behind him. "That crazy son of a chicken thinks Sophie got sick because of the fae." He rummaged through the refrigerator for the last of the beer, cracking open the can with a hiss. "Turn it up; let's hear what he has to say." He crossed into the living room and dropped down onto the sofa beside Toby, propping his feet up on the table scuffed from his boots.

"We were so lucky to get her into the clinical trial, and the new treatment was working. She was feeling better, and it was only a matter of time before she got to come home. We were hoping for another remission."

"Not likely." Xavier scoffed. "Poor Sophie was dying, and he was only prolonging her suffering."

"Did you know she was missing?" Toby glanced at Xavier's profile in the fading light of the sunset outside the window.

"We heard about it just this morning. She disappeared from her hospital room a few days ago. So Claude Devereaux would have everyone believe."

"You don't believe him?" Toby asked.

He shook his head, a sad look on his face. "She was really sick, Toby. I think she died, and he's trying to blame it on us."

"How could a father do that?" Toby couldn't imagine his

own father using the death of one of his children for ... political gain. It didn't make any sense.

"Let's see what story he's come up with." Xavier nodded toward the television.

"My girl was so happy." Claude's eyes filled with tears. "She was about to get married. She was so excited for the wedding to her childhood sweetheart."

"Ha!" Xavier snorted. "Soph couldn't stand that idiot brother of mine and their sham of an engagement."

"I forgot Gabe was your half-brother." Xavier and Gabe's mother was human, but Xavier's father was one of the few full fae in the human realm, and Gabe's father was about as human as they came. Gabe was the oldest of the two, and Toby suspected their mother had married Xavier's fae father once Gabe's father died in the darkness. That had to be a big part of why the two hated each other so much. It couldn't just be about Xavier's magic. Not that he had much to speak of.

"When did you last see your daughter, Mr. Devereaux?" the host asked in a hushed tone.

"The night she was taken. I left her sleeping peacefully. The nurse told me it was a good time to go home for a shower and some rest." He fidgeted in his seat, staring off into the audience with unseeing eyes. "I barely left her side the whole time she was in the hospital. But that nurse ... the male nurse she'd befriended—the one giving her the treatment. I swear, he was fae, and he was trying to get me to leave my daughter so they could take her."

"And why would they want her?"

"They know I'd do anything for my Sophie-Ann." Claude swiped a hand across his eyes. "They knew it would cripple me ... to lose my girl when she was so sick. To deprive her of the medicine that was keeping her alive."

"I'm so sorry for the pain you're dealing with, Claude."

The host laid a comforting hand on his shoulder. "I hate to play devil's advocate, but there are rumors. Rumors that say your Sophie-Ann died in the hospital and this accusation of a fae abduction is your attempt to make headlines. To push your agenda."

"That's a lie! Sophie-Ann Devereaux is not dead. And I can prove it."

"How?" The host's eyes sparkled with excitement. "How can you prove such a thing?"

"We have a witness who saw it all happen."

"What did this witness see?"

"A boy. A fae boy ... one I stupidly trusted. He was the one with her when she collapsed, and he got her the help she needed. I let him visit her as much as he wanted." Claude shook his head. "That's the problem with the fae among us. You can't tell what they are until it's too late."

"And this boy just led your deathly sick daughter from the hospital without anyone stopping them?" The host gazed across her audience, an incredulous look on her face and a tone of disbelief in her voice.

"No." Claude shook his head. "This boy had help. An older fae man was with him this time—the one in all the papers. I'd never seen them together before. I even had my people watching over this kid, thinking he needed protection from all the fae out there." He snorted in disgust.

"This man opened some kind of ... magical doorway. Our witness saw it with their own eyes. A seam of violet light split the air, and the boy took my girl from her bed, stepped into that light, and just ... vanished."

"Vanished?" the woman whispered. "Where do you think they went, Mr. Devereaux?"

"That fae boy took my daughter to their world. Our witness heard them talking about a place called Lenya."

"For what purpose?"

Claude Devereaux sat up straight, pulling his shoulders back as he stared at the camera. "To start a war."

Toby shot out of his seat. "I'm going to kill him."

"Easier said than done." Xavier leaned forward, setting his empty beer can on the table. "We've been trying to get close enough to Claude Devereaux to kill him for years. He's surrounded by HAFS people day and night."

"I'm not talking about this idiot." Toby gestured at the screen. "When I see Gulliver O'Shea again, I'm going to strangle him with that blasted tail of his."

"Gulliver? What's he got to do with this?"

"Who do you think took Sophie to Lenya?" Toby's head throbbed harder as he paced the length of the tiny room. "I'm going to kill him. No ... I'll never get a chance to. *Tia's* going to kill him."

"What's a Lenya?"

"It's one of the five kingdoms," Toby said absently.

"I always thought there were only three, and then Gulliver said there was a place called Myrkur, where he's from, so that makes four."

"We just found out about Lenya. Long story." A jolt of sorrow hit him so hard that he faltered in his steps. Toby could never think about Lenya without seeing the expression on Logan's face the moment he died on the fire plains.

Toby closed his eyes, pushing thoughts of the man he should have spent the rest of his life with to the back of his mind.

"I didn't think Gulliver had magic. I know he's an O'Shea by adoption, but how did he open a portal?" Xavier asked.

"He didn't. Uncle Griff did. And he didn't tell me. Why would he not tell me?" Toby raked a hand through his hair in frustration. "Ow!" The bandage covering his shoulder pulled away from the skin, tugging on the stitches the half-fae healer had used to sew his arm back together.

"Watch out, you're going to rip your stitches." Xavier moved to his side, forcing him to sit back on the couch and take it easy.

A wave of dizziness washed over Toby, and he sank down onto the cushions. "He's just made everything so much worse." He reached up with his uninjured hand to scratch the itchy wound beneath his t-shirt, and Xavier slapped his hand away.

"Stop that, you'll get your germs all over it." He tugged Toby's sleeve down and studied the wound with a frown. "Stay right there; we're cleaning this again." He went to the kitchen to retrieve his healing kit.

"Just slap a fresh bandage on it. We've got bigger things to deal with." Like murdering a certain dark fae for taking a human to the healing pools in Lenya. He was almost certain that was what Gulliver meant to do with the sick Sophie. If she was truly on death's door as Xavier claimed, then Toby knew Gulliver was desperate enough to try anything to save her life. Even taking a human to the healing pools the leaders of the five kingdoms had recently ruled to be used only in the gravest of situations, and only with the consent of all five kingdoms.

Gulliver's heart was in the right place, but Toby feared Claude Devereaux was right. He'd just started a war. One that could destroy everything.

"Sit still. This wound isn't faring well, and if you don't want to end up in the hospital yourself, you're going to let me clean it as often as it needs cleaning. Now take your shirt off."

Toby winced at the bowl of hot water Xavier set on the side table. "Fine. Just be quick about it." He tugged the shirt over his head with one arm.

"Healer Maddox sent over a new poultice for you. He doesn't have much magic, but his potions always work." Xavier leaned over him, pressing a steaming hot cloth over the still swollen wound.

"Ouch. That's really hot." Toby pulled away.

"Don't be a baby. The heat will help with the swelling."

"What's that horrible smell?" Toby's nose wrinkled at the awful scent of rotted eggs and other dead things.

"The poultice." Xavier poured rubbing alcohol over his hands and dribbled some onto a clean paper towel. "Hold still. This is the part that hurts." He removed the warm cloth and dabbed at Toby's stitches.

"Watch it, that stings!" Toby pulled away again, but Xavier wouldn't let him.

"It's supposed to. That means it's working."

"By eating off my skin?" Toby winced.

Xavier chuckled. "The big and mighty prince of fae is scared of a little alcohol."

"Well, where I come from, we drink the alcohol, not bathe in it," Toby growled. "And I'm not the prince of fae. I'm just a magicless fae prince. There's a difference."

"Well, we don't have fae princes here. Here we're all just fae." He gently swabbed the wound until he was satisfied it was clean enough.

"I think that's why I like it here," Toby muttered. "Here, it doesn't matter what you can and can't do with magic."

"Huh." Xavier studied Toby's shoulder for a moment before he took up the jar of foul-smelling stuff.

"What's that mean?"

"What?"

"Your 'huh'. You say it like you've got something more to say."

"It's just ... it hasn't escaped me that your sister queen—

the one with all the magic—sent two fae with very little magic between them to investigate what's happening to the fae here."

"What of it?" Toby shrugged. "We blend in better. That's all."

"Huh." Xavier bit his bottom lip as he dabbed the muddy poultice over Toby's stitches.

"Now, what?"

"I guess it seems like she probably had more of a reason for sending you two than just your ability to blend in. From what you've told me, any fae can come here and humans will only see them as human as long as they use their glamour. Even Dark Fae like Gullie can look like humans here. So, maybe your queen thinks the fae with the least magic are just as capable as those with all the magic you lack."

"Tia would never judge anyone as less for not having magic." Toby lifted his chin.

"That's ... interesting. Not at all what I would have expected from such a powerful queen."

"Ugh, that can't possibly be good for the germs you keep talking about." Toby plugged his nose to avoid the awful reek coming from his arm. "Am I going to have to walk around smelling like an outhouse?"

"Afraid so. At least until the swelling goes down." Xavier wrapped a clean bandage around Toby's shoulder. "But this is powerful stuff. At least on this side of the veil between worlds. I'm sure your fae healers back home could have you fixed up in no time."

"Not necessarily. There are some magical things that can aid healing, but for the most part, this isn't all that much different than it is at home."

"They just don't smell as bad?" A smile tugged at the corners of Xavier's perfect mouth.

"Yeah, but the smelly ones are usually the ones you have to drink." Toby gave him a hesitant smile.

"All right." Xavier hopped to his feet to clean up the old bandages. "We've got to get to a meeting later tonight." He moved into the kitchen to wash his hands and toss the rubbish into the trash bin.

"What for?" Toby followed him, sitting on one of the bar stools at the two-seater counter that made up the bulk of the kitchen.

"HAFS is about to make a big move. Maybe their biggest yet in light of Sophie's abduction."

"She wasn't abducted. At least, not maliciously."

"What was Gullie thinking by taking her to the fae realm?" Xavier shook his head.

"Some of that healing magic we don't have that much of." Toby let out a weary sigh. "I'll tell you all about it later. What's HAFS planning?"

Xavier retrieved a bottle of spirits he kept in the freezer and poured them each a drink. "We have fae villages all over the world. We mostly live in small groups in rural areas so we don't call that much attention to ourselves."

Toby gave a mirthless laugh at that. "When we first came here, we thought it was just the one community in New Orleans."

"Well, just like us, HAFS has groups all over the world, and just like us, they are banding together to go after the largest fae settlement in the world."

"Where is that?"

"A place called Los Angeles. It's a huge city about two thousand miles from here."

"And this city is all fae?" Toby asked. He didn't know how far two thousand miles was, but he could imagine it wasn't close.

"No, not entirely, but there are thousands of fae living among the humans there. It's sort of a strange place even for humans. The people there are more accepting of those different from themselves."

"And HAFS is going to attack?"

"Not just attack." Xavier sighed, knocking back the contents of the small glass he'd poured for each of them. Toby quickly followed suit, imagining he needed the fortification for what Xavier was about to reveal. "According to our intel there in L.A., the head of all of HAFS is calling in every member from across the country to assist in the raid on the city. We suspect they're going to try to blow the entire city off the map, and we've got to figure out a way to mobilize there quickly enough to do something about it."

Toby reached for the bottle and poured them another drink. "I might have a way we can do that." He let out a worried sigh before he tipped the clear contents of the small glass into his mouth with a wince. "But there's someone I need to talk to first."

Chapter Eight
SOPHIE-ANN

This infernal castle was freezing. Sophie huddled under her blankets in the oh-so-comfortable feather bed in her huge room in a fantasy fae palace in the coldest lands she'd ever visited. Not that she'd ever traveled anywhere remotely interesting.

She'd never admit it to a living soul, but Iskalt was gorgeous. A land of ice and snow surrounded by majestic mountains, blue skies, and cute villages, Iskalt was a veritable winter wonderland. Sophie would give just about anything to explore more of the idyllic countryside she could see from her balcony window, but she wasn't here on vacation. She was here against her will, and she would never forgive Gulliver for dragging her through another portal.

She didn't understand why they'd taken her to the human realm for a brief stay at the Ohio farmhouse before they traveled by portal to this snowy realm. If she could have gotten away from these fracking fae people there, she could have made her way back to New Orleans.

She rolled onto her side, gazing at the cheery fire cracking in her fireplace. It was magic. Had to be. She'd watched the fire for hours, and it never died down. Never needed more wood. The room itself was warm, and her bed was toasty with soft fur blankets piled on top of her, but the chill she felt came from the inside.

Ever since she woke from the healing pools, Sophie was restless, and a constant chill had settled deep in her bones, as if the magic that had healed her lingered within.

She shoved the blankets aside and grabbed the dressing robe they'd given her to wear over her clothes. She couldn't stay in bed for another minute. Her mind and traitorous body couldn't seem to forget the sensation of so much power rushing through her. Just the thought of it now left her frightened. Frightened of her innermost private thoughts—the ones that admitted to enjoying the touch of magic. The thoughts that yearned to feel it again.

"Enough." Sophie stuffed her feet into slippers warming by the fire. Tossing the robe over her shoulders, she decided to go exploring. Surely there were enough interesting things to see in this castle to keep her occupied until she grew tired enough to sleep.

She wandered along the wide hallway, her slippered feet whispering against the cold stone floors. She studied the old tapestries covering the walls, keeping the chill at bay. Each was a sweeping canvas of history painted in needlepoint, depicting battles of long-forgotten wars. Newer tapestries illustrated times of peace and unity among the kingdoms. Sophie stopped to study a landscape of a valley, half shrouded in darkness and half bathed in brilliant sunlight. Both sides of the valley were beautiful in their own way. Even the darkness seemed friendly and inviting, with its shades of violet and a purple so dark it was almost black.

Dark red flowers bloomed in the moonlight right alongside bright white blossoms bobbing in the breeze under the shining sun. On the hill overlooking the valley stood three children of about the same age. A girl with wild strawberry blond hair and a little boy that looked a lot like her. Sophie wondered if this was the queen with her twin brother.

Standing between them was a skinny boy, slightly taller than the twins with knobby knees and dark hair that stood up on end. His tail seemed so natural in this setting; the leaf-shaped tip laid on the girl's shoulder like a human would drape an arm around a friend.

Sophie reached to touch the tapestry, knowing without a doubt if the three children could turn around to face her, one would have the most remarkable cat-like eyes. "Gullie," she whispered, still trying to resolve the image she had of him and his human features with the odd fae features of the man she'd grown to like despite her better judgment. It was thanks to him that she was still here. Still breathing. He was the reason she felt stronger now than she ever had before.

But magic had healed her, and Sophie Devereaux did not trust magic nor the creatures that wielded it.

Leaving her conflicting thoughts behind with the tapestry, Sophie explored the rest of the hall and followed a winding stone stairway up to a tower with circular rooms. Each level revealed a different room. The first was a cheerful warm sitting room that had the look of a well-loved corner of the castle. The second level revealed a room of windows. A solarium with the most spectacular views of the lake and the silvery expanse of snow fields in the moonlight. Sophie stayed there for the longest time, just enjoying the view.

Heavy footsteps echoed overhead, followed by the sound of a slamming door. Intrigued by the silence that followed, Sophie made her way up to the third level of the tower to find a wide-open room with doorways leading to other parts of the castle. The walls here were covered in an array of swords and shields. Even an ancient set of armor stood under a tartan banner of aged dark blue and pale green plaid.

A crash of steel caught her attention, and she went looking for the culprit. Something told her she should go back to her room, but she needed to know who else was up on this restless night. Sophie tiptoed to a door left cracked open.

Cold air rushed in her face as she peeked through the gap. It was a courtyard, high above the rest of the castle, like a bridge between turret towers.

A lone figure raced across the bridge amid the quiet snowfall, his sword glinting in the moonlight and his tail lashing out behind him.

Gulliver. Even among the fae, he was unusual. During her time here in Iskalt, she'd met all manner of creatures. Some with wings and others with horns like beasts of the land. She'd even caught sight of an enormous creature she was almost certain was an ogre. Her father would call them vile devils, but they'd all been nothing but kind to Sophie since her arrival. She'd yet to meet a single fae who wasn't kind. Yet, they had magic that could destroy the human world.

Gulliver moved gracefully, fluid and sure as he practiced with his sword, like a warrior who'd trained all his life with a blade in his hand. Gone was the awkward geek who ate baskets of beignets and said the most ridiculous things.

Tonight, he seemed as though he fought demons of his own, his sword arcing through the air to strike imagined enemies, slaying the shadows of doubt and frustration that plagued his mind.

A gust of wind swept across the courtyard, and Sophie

yelped at the bite of snow and ice that billowed in her face through the crack in the door.

Clapping a hand over her mouth, she took a step back, but he'd already seen her.

"Sophie?" Gulliver dropped his sword at his side.

Sophie didn't stick around for him to ask her what she was doing out of bed. Like a coward, she turned and ran through the nearest door and down a flight of stairs, leaving the tower and its beautiful circular rooms behind.

Sophie darted into a room at the end of the short hallway and closed it behind her, leaning against it. She sucked in a deep breath, urging her heart to slow its pounding in her chest.

"Sophie?" Gulliver's voice reached her ears. Stifling a groan, she moved across the large room, realizing it was a library filled with rows and rows of books, the domed ceiling letting in the moonlight as she gazed around, breathless. It was the most beautiful room she'd ever seen.

"Sophie?" Gulliver stepped into the room, studying Sophie's face. She'd forgotten to hide. Through all the years of her illness, books were her sole companion. She escaped the daily grind of getting out of bed, faking her way through the motions of life until she couldn't take it anymore, and escaped it all through the pages of a book. "Are you all right?"

Sophie nodded. "It's so beautiful." She turned in a circle, taking it all in. The cold fireplace at the center of the room was surrounded by well-worn leather chairs. Soft rugs covered the floors and lamplight illuminated each aisle of books, coming to life as she moved closer.

"This is Tia's favorite room in the castle." Gulliver followed. "I've never been much of a reader, but when we were kids, we came here on the coldest days. She and Toby would read all the human tales while I carved some of the characters they described." Gulliver crossed the room to the fireplace, and flames erupted at his movement. "Here, check this out." He lifted a small figurine from the mantle.

"Is that ... a hippogriff?" Sophie almost laughed until she realized they might actually have such terrifying creatures in Iskalt.

"Buckbeak from *Harry Potter*." Gulliver smiled, placing the heavy figure in her hand. "Brea and Tia loved reading those books over and over. Tia gets a kick out of the humans' imagination for magic. I even carved her a wand she carried around for nearly a year when she was twelve."

"I imagine lots of people have wands here," Sophie blurted.

"No." Gulliver shook his head. "Real magic doesn't work that way. It takes a lot more than wand waving and memorizing spells to create magic."

"Magic scares me." Sophie didn't know why she said it. But with Gulliver, she always found herself being honest with her feelings.

"It used to scare me too." Gulliver placed the figurine back on the mantle. "I grew up without magic, just like you. When I first saw real magic—the kind used in warfare—it terrified me."

"Magical warfare?" Sophie shivered at the thought of such power turned against her people.

"Thankfully we are at peace now. For the first time in generations, all five kingdoms are not only at peace with one another, but we are all genuinely friends, eager for a long and happy future without war."

Sophie moved to look at all the delicate carvings adorning the mantle, so much like the magnolia carving Gullie had made for her. She saw lots of familiar characters from *Harry Potter* and *Game of Thrones*. She even saw a hobbit and five golden rings perched on a wooden stand. Such familiar sights made her smile. It made Gulliver seem that much more ... human. Despite his tail and eyes that marked him as fae.

"This library is amazing." She picked up a book from a side table, where someone had recently discarded it. "*Dune*?" She laughed. "I just read this a few weeks ago." She set it back down.

"King Lochlan ... well, former King Lochlan loves human fantasy and science fiction," Gulliver said. "Most of the human books here are ones he's collected over the years."

Sophie wandered over to a row of leather-bound books on a nearby shelf. She studied the titles. "Human tales?" She lifted her gaze to Gulliver.

"There are hundreds of them. Stories much like your fairy tales."

"Oh. I see." She smiled, turning in a circle to take in the glorious library she could get lost in. "It's just like in *Beauty and the Beast*."

"The beast?" Gulliver's voice took on a hard edge. "I suppose that makes me the beast."

She looked up in surprise, horrified by what she'd said. Of course, he wouldn't get the reference to the library. "No, that's not—"

"It's fine. I'm used to it." Gulliver turned, his tail dragging lifelessly behind him. "I'll just leave you to explore. Though, you should probably think about getting some sleep soon." He stood at the doorway, his back to her. "Just take the hall to the left and you'll find the main stairs. Go up one floor and your room is down the hall to the right. In case you weren't sure how to get back."

With that he left, shutting the door behind him.

Sophie started to follow. She got as far as the door before she stopped. She didn't know what to say to him. She hadn't meant to call him a beast, and she felt awful about it. She didn't see him that way at all. His features were alarming at first, but she was getting used to seeing his true form. His tail suited him, and to her, he was just Gulliver. The kindest man she'd ever met. He'd never mistreated her. Nor had any of his fae friends.

Gulliver O'Shea had saved her life, and she was certain he was in a lot of trouble for taking such a huge risk, bringing a human to his world. And she knew he'd do it all over again just to give her a chance at the life he claimed should have been hers all along.

"Sophie-Ann Devereaux, maybe it's high time you actually learn something about these people before you go judging them all by your father's opinions." Sophie turned back to the library and began searching for answers.

Chapter Nine
GULLIVER

It had been a long time since Gulliver felt self-conscious about the way he looked. Sure, he got stares wherever he went outside Myrkur, but those closest to him never made him feel different. Tia and Toby had been his best and only friends for so much of his life. To them, he was just Gullie.

And yet, that word. He'd heard it before. Beast.

Maybe that was truly what he was. A creature not meant for civilized life. It was how Sophie would always see him. No matter how much he cared about her, she could never truly care for him.

He rolled over in bed, squeezing his eyes shut. "Sleep, Gulliver," he muttered. "You idiot."

But sleep refused to come. That blissful darkness only got louder and louder, a void shouting in his mind.

Beast.

He flopped onto his back, shifting when his tail got stuck.

Running a hand down the length of it, he tried to remember the boy who'd never questioned his identity. The one who knew this tail was as much a part of what made him Gulliver as anything else.

"I'm sorry," he whispered, his fingers drifting over the tiny hairs. "You know I don't hate you. Sometimes, I just wish everyone else could love you as much as I do."

Snickering came from the door Gulliver hadn't heard open, a familiar sound.

"Were you just talking to your tail?" Tia's laughter cut through the dark.

"No." Gulliver sat up. "Do you always creep around in the dark like a creep?"

He could practically hear her grin. "Nice use of the human word, but you didn't need to use it twice in the same sentence."

"At least I got it right this time."

"Yeah, but it was pretty funny when you called your mom a creep just for hugging you."

"Don't remind me." He groaned. His mom sometimes didn't have the greatest sense of humor. She took everything so literally, and Brea had already explained to the entire family what a creep was. That didn't go over so well.

Tia walked farther into the room, stopping at the hearth. "*Dóiteán*." Flames spread in the cold ashes, casting the marble in an orange glow.

"Is there something you want?" A chill raced through Gulliver, and he pulled the covers up to his bare chest. "I was sleeping, you know."

"Like I'm going to believe that."

"It's the middle of the night. Why wouldn't I be sleeping?" Between Keir last night and now Tia tonight, he'd never get any rest.

She crawled onto the bed, pulling back the covers so she could burrow underneath at his side.

"Help yourself." He rolled his eyes.

"Thanks. I will." She leaned back against the feather pillows. "Now, to answer your question ... you're staying next door to a woman you lurve."

"I what?"

"Lurve."

"Stop that."

"Stop what?"

Did she always have to be obnoxious? "Stop saying that. I don't love her."

"I didn't say you did. I believe I said *lurve*."

"Well, I don't."

"You don't what?" She turned onto her side to look at him.

He sighed. "Lurve her."

"Don't be ridiculous, Gulliver freakydeaky O'Shea. Lurve isn't a word."

He was going to strangle her. "You know I don't have a middle name."

"Of course you do; I gave you one when you were twelve."

"That one doesn't count."

"Yes, it does, Gulliver Alexander O'Shea."

"That's better." Gullie grinned into the darkness.

"Ugh, you just wanted me to say it."

"Of course."

A knock at the door drew their attention, but Gulliver already knew who it would be. Where one annoying royal went ... "Come in, Keir."

Keir entered more cautiously, at least pretending he didn't want to invade Gulliver's space a second night in a row. In reality, he'd become way too much like Tia in the last year. "I thought my wife might be here."

"Guys," Gulliver whined, "it's the middle of the night."

"Right." Tia nodded, as if she completely understood. "Keir is probably tired too." She lifted the edge of the blankets and scooted closer to Gulliver.

Keir kicked off his shoes and slid in next to his wife.

Gulliver rubbed his eyes. "And just why are the queen and king in my bed?"

"You make it sound so wrong." Tia pouted.

"It is wrong. Please go."

"Maybe we should leave him alone," Keir whispered.

Tia ignored him. "Can't I just want to talk to my best friend?"

"No. Not in the middle of the night. And not in my bed."

"Don't be mean." She reached over and pinched him.

Gulliver yelped. "Keir, tell her to stop."

The king rubbed his eyes. "Have you ever once known her to listen to me?"

"He has a point." She jabbed a thumb Keir's way.

Gulliver sank down lower in his bed. Just a few minutes ago, he'd been unable to sleep, and now, all he wanted to do was close his eyes and make the world disappear, make obnoxious royals disappear.

Wanting the attention off him and his dark thoughts, Gulliver turned onto his side to face Tia. "Have you thought about what we're going to do?"

She'd had meetings with representatives from each of the other kingdoms in the last day. He'd wanted to join her, but she didn't let him, saying he was too close to what was going on in the human world. That scared him. It told him whatever plan she'd started crafting, it wouldn't be good for the humans.

Tia and Keir shared a look he didn't trust. "We're here to talk about you, Gul."

"What aren't you saying?" He could see it on her face. Guilt.

"We've been developing a new plan, but I'm not ready to share it yet. Can you just trust me?"

"Tia, I trust you more than I trust myself sometimes. But this is an entire world of humans we're talking about. You can't go all O'Shea on this."

"What's that supposed to mean?"

Keir was the one who answered. "Your entire family has a bit of an impulse problem, love."

"We absolutely do not."

Gulliver and Keir shared a disbelieving look. Lochlan, Griff ... not to mention their mother, the woman who once stole the most powerful book in the world. The only O'Shea Gulliver once considered calm and logical was Toby, but that was out the window now.

"Whatever you say." Gulliver stared at the dark ceiling. "We done here? Some of us would like to get some sleep ... without all of the Iskalt palace in his bed."

Keir started to leave, but Tia clutched his arm, forcing him to stay. "No. Something is wrong."

"What?" He sat up so quickly his head swam. "Is Sophie okay?"

"I'm going to ignore that she was the first one you thought of, despite the fact you apparently don't lurve her. No, you fool." She slapped the side of his head. "Something is wrong with you."

He shoved her hand away when she tried to hit him again. "Thanks for that, but I'm fine."

"You are not. Keir told me you were training tonight. You

only do that when whatever is on your mind is worse than the exercise."

"You make me sound like a lazy oaf."

She sighed. "You would just rather play in the snow or pick winter berries than work up a sweat."

Okay, maybe she had a point.

"I have a lot on my mind." And the worst of it was from after he worked with the sword.

She tapped her lips. "Does that explain why you were talking to your tail?"

Keir laughed. "He was what now?"

"Literally talking to it. Like it was a sentient thing."

Gulliver ran a hand down the length of it. "She doesn't mean it, little Gulliver."

"Please don't tell me that's really its name." Keir choked on a laugh.

"Wouldn't you like to know?" It wasn't, but he owed them no answers. If he wanted to talk to his tail, he could.

"I would like to know." Keir looked so confused it was almost comical. "That's why I asked."

"Babe." Tia laid a gentle hand on his chest. "It's a human saying that basically means you're out of luck because he isn't going to tell you."

"Then, why didn't he just say that?" He shook his head. "I will never understand you two and your human phrases."

"Good." She smirked. "Best friends have to have their secret language that husbands can't decipher."

"Uh, Tia." Gulliver couldn't stop his smile. "It's not exactly secret if an entire world of humans understands."

"Stop with the logic, Gulliver," Keir said. "Tia doesn't like it."

She pinched him, but he notably didn't yelp as Gulliver had. Freaking Lenyans and their toughness.

Gulliver drew in a deep breath, thankful that for a few moments, Tia had distracted him from the word circulating in his mind.

Beast.

Beast.

Beast.

He was a beast, according to Sophie.

They all went silent, even Tia, their breath the only sound between them. As much as Gulliver protested it, he liked having the pair with him. Yes, even in his bed. Tia was his best friend, his other half. They were meant to be together forever, in a purely platonic way. And Keir ... as grumpy as he could be, Gulliver trusted him. Somehow, after everything that happened all that time ago in Lenya, Keir and he had become ... friends?

After a while, a soft snore broke the silence and then a giggle.

"Is he ...?" Gulliver didn't need to finish the question. Keir was asleep. In Gulliver's bed.

Tia nodded, slapping a hand over her mouth.

Keir snorted, making them both jump, and then snored again. Another sound soon joined in, like rushing air.

"Oh no." Tia scooted away from her husband, pressing into Gulliver, her entire body shaking with laughter.

"What?" Then, he smelled it. "He's dying." He scrambled from the bed, falling to the soft carpet spread underneath. The smell followed him.

Tia tumbled out next to him. "Rotting from the inside out."

"That's horrid."

The two of them crawled off the carpet and across the stone until they reached the wall next to the hearth. They leaned against the cool marble, gasping for breath.

"That was awful." Tia bent over, laughing.

"You're the one who married the man."

"Because I lurve him."

He stared at her. "What's it like to be loved back?"

That sobered her, and she sat up straighter. "It's ... confusing."

"That was not what I was expecting."

"My whole life, I've heard all these things about myself. I was wild, uncontrollable, reckless. Gullie, I saved an entire kingdom, and still, everyone was always just waiting for me to mess up. And when I did, it proved them right."

"No, you—"

"I'm answering your question. From the moment I met Keir, he saw me as a formidable foe. When he finally stopped hating me, he didn't lose that respect. In his eyes, I'm capable. He believes in me as I never believed in myself. Like when all the fae in the human realm need my help and I can't figure out how. I'm not sure why he still has faith other than the fact that he loves me. That's why it's confusing."

"It sounds wonderful."

"Oh, it is." Her smile dropped. "Gul, I know something is wrong."

He opened his mouth to speak, but she cut him off.

"Sometimes, I feel like I know you more than I know myself. I can tell when that dark cloud you get is growing. It's not just your normal self-consciousness. What happened? If you tell me again that it's nothing, that you're fine, I'm going to light your entire room on fire."

"In your own castle?"

"Yes. Because I care more about you than I do about a stupid castle. Speak."

A sigh rattled from his lungs. "I'm a beast."

She laughed suddenly and loud before clapping a hand

over her mouth. "I'm sorry. I just was not expecting that. What do you mean?"

He told her about Sophie finding him, about the library, and how he assumed they were finally getting along. "Then, she called me a beast."

Tia looped her arm through his, shifting so they were leaning against each other, holding each other up. "What exactly did she say?"

"She said she was a beauty, and I was a beast."

Tia fell quiet, and it took Gulliver a moment to realize she was grinning. "Gul."

"What?" He was starting to lose patience with her.

"Oh, Gullie, Gullie, Gullie." She shook her head. "You, my dear friend, need to read more human tales."

"What are you talking about?"

"It's a story. *Beauty and the Beast.* A young woman falls in love with a man who has been cursed to live in the body of a beast. In his castle he had a fabulous library and she loved to read."

"Oh." Gulliver frowned. "I'm not sure that makes it any better. I'm not cursed and that wasn't my library. This is just me."

"Of course it's you. And what you are is magnificent. If she calls you a beast again, I'm going to ... cut her hair with my magic or something."

"Vicious." He bumped her shoulder.

"Shut up. I don't want to actually hurt the human, but girls love their hair. Anyway, there's something you don't understand about *Beauty and the Beast.*"

A loud and sudden snore came from the bed, and they both looked Keir's way. That had to have woken him up, but he continued to sleep.

"What don't I understand?" Gulliver drew Tia's attention back to him.

She rested her head on his shoulder. "That story has a happy ending."

Chapter Ten
TOBY

This was a bad idea.

Or the best idea he'd ever had.

Toby wasn't quite sure which, but he knew his family was going to be furious either way.

"I still don't understand what we're waiting for." Xavier paced the length of the room. He reminded Toby of Tia with his inability to sit still, his need to be constantly in motion, to know what was happening at all times.

"Then, why are you nervous?" A smile tugged at Toby's lips. He wouldn't admit it, but he found Xavier kind of adorable.

"Because ..." Xavier stopped and blew out a breath. "I have a feeling whatever you've done is going to change everything."

"That's because it is." Toby stood, his lips stretching into a full-blown grin. "I went to see my grandfather."

"Your ..." Xavier rubbed the back of his neck. "I'm

confused. How is an old man supposed to help us save an entire city full of fae?"

"Don't let him hear you call him old. Besides, my grandfather ... he's not like others."

"Wait, you're a prince. He's ..." Xavier's eyes widened.

"No. He's my mother's father, so he's not of Iskalt. But he was once the King of Fargelsi." Toby shrugged. "Until his sister locked him away for about eighteen years in a magical dungeon. My mom broke him out, but he didn't want his kingdom back. His illegitimate daughter is now the queen there. She rules with her human husband."

Xavier's eyes went so big they looked like they'd fall right out of his head. "There's a human sitting on a fae throne?"

"Two, actually. My aunt Alona, the Queen of Eldur, is human. But that's not important. What is important is that we need to go."

"Where?"

Toby wasn't sure how to explain Aghadoon to someone who'd only ever seen the much-weakened magic of the half-fae living in the human realm. "My grandfather is going to meet us." It was better if the fae here just saw it. Plus, part of him wanted to see the looks on their faces when a village seemed to just drop out of the sky.

Maybe he was more like his sister than he cared to admit.

That thought sobered him. He'd never let her know this, but he missed her. He hated that she was probably angry with him for staying, angry that he'd involved himself in a war between the humans and the fae. At first, he'd hoped HAFS was just a fringe group that could be beaten easily without risking a war.

Now, he knew the truth. They had to fight for this world.

Xavier was looking at him expectantly, head cocked to the side. He opened his mouth to say something, but a flash of violet light cut him off, and he jumped back, flattening himself against the wall of the makeshift bedroom.

Toby sighed. Here it comes.

Griffin stepped through the portal in a wave of anger, advancing on Toby. So, that answered that question. He knew. Of course Grandfather would get a message to him. Toby had been a fool to think he'd keep it to himself.

"What did you do?" Griff roared.

Toby refused to cower in the face of his uncle. It was rare that Griffin showed his anger over the last few years. He was usually the one calming Father, making sure he didn't go completely to the dark side. Tia would be proud of that human reference.

"What are you smiling about, boy?" Griff's old tactic was still in play. The few times he did get mad, he made those around him feel like children. Namely, his son.

But Toby wasn't Gulliver. He wasn't even the Toby everyone back home knew. That fae died when Logan did. Now, he was a fae with nothing left to lose, one who didn't back down any longer.

"I'm smiling because it's done, uncle. You can't stop it now."

"Like magic, I can't!"

"I'd like to see you try to change Grandfather's mind when it's made up." Not only that, but his grandfather would never obey Griffin. He'd never fully trusted him again after Griffin worked for Regan during the years he was imprisoned. He'd forgiven him, but he'd never forgotten.

Griffin cursed. "Aghadoon is no longer meant to exist in the human realm. It's too dangerous."

"Why?" Toby stepped toward him. "Because it could reveal our existence to the humans? Guess what. They know about us. We're no longer a secret. Our world is no longer a secret. And this is what happens when they see us. They come for us, hunting us down in the very streets we've lived on our whole lives."

"You lived in Iskalt most of your life."

"Yes, but Xavier hasn't. Every other fae or half-fae who is part of this movement hasn't. They've never set foot in Iskalt. This is their world as much as the humans. Yet, they're also our fae. We owe it to them to make sure they can live their lives peacefully in the place of their choosing."

Griffin's anger faded away, and his shoulders dropped. "You still think that's possible? The humans will never stop."

"I don't know what's possible, only that we have to try. Aghadoon is our best shot to reach Lost Angelica in time. I've never been there so I can't open a portal."

"Los Angeles," Xavier cut in.

"Yeah, that."

Griffin sighed. "Where is he meeting you?"

The triumph didn't feel good this time. He was glad his uncle supported him, but he wished they hadn't needed to resort to Aghadoon in the first place. "There's a park near here. It's used for some human game."

"Soccer fields," Xavier explained. "Toby said his grandfather needed a wide-open space, though I'm still not sure why."

Griffin leveled Toby with a look. "You didn't tell him?"

Toby gave him a sheepish smile. "Please let me have my fun."

"You are my kid, aren't you?"

It was a fact rarely spoken of, but Tia had always been the risk taker like Griff. Toby was the opposite. Except lately.

"Wait." Xavier looked between them, confusion creasing his brow.

Toby grabbed his arm and started pulling him toward the

door. "Long story. Maybe I'll tell you someday." If they made it through this, he wanted to tell Xavier everything. It hurt to admit that, made his heart ache for the one man who'd known him completely.

But Logan was gone. He wasn't coming back. And Toby had a long life ahead of him. He didn't want to spend the rest of it in pain, living in the past.

When they got to the soccer fields, it was raining, soaking the ground and turning parts of it into mud. Toby's boots stuck, and he had to pull them free with each step.

He'd never seen as much rain as he had since being in the human realm. In Iskalt, they got lots of snow. Eldur was mostly heat. They'd have basked in this kind of weather. Fargelsi got rain, but not nearly this much.

"There's nothing here." Xavier crossed his arms on his chest and peered across the fields. "Where's your grandfather?"

Griffin blew drops of water off his lips. "Just wait, kid." He shook his head. "I can't believe Toby didn't prepare you for this."

Toby looked at the people behind them, the leadership of their group of rebels. They'd insisted on coming to any sort of meeting, and Toby had no way of stopping them. There must have been twenty half-fae and human allies waiting for something they didn't understand.

"What time is it?" Toby asked.

Xavier pulled out his phone. "One."

"He's late." Grandfather was supposed to arrive ten minutes ago. Had something happened? Did Tia stop him? Or one of the other royals? Brandon O'Rourke was beyond the rule of any kingdom. He made his own decisions and was never late. He listened to the council of kings and queens, but he did not always obey them.

That was why he'd agreed to come here.

It began with a glint of light at the furthest edge of the field, where the open space gave way to beautiful oak trees that stretched toward the sky. The trees started to bend, as if shrinking away from an oncoming storm that would crush them where they stood.

A curse floated on the air—Xavier's only word as two pillars appeared as if from nothing. The rest of the village stayed hidden, but Toby knew it was there. Calm settled in him. Aghadoon was a piece of home. He hadn't visited the village much in the years since he spent way too long there during the battle of Myrkur.

A young man who looked to be in his thirties strolled through the pillars. Toby cast a glance toward Xavier, taking in the shock on his face, the way he looked frozen to the spot.

Totally worth the secrecy.

Griffin rolled his eyes at Toby's glee and walked forward to meet Brandon. The two men shook hands before Brandon turned to Toby, his face softening. "You have a lot of fae worried, young man." He pulled Toby into a hug. "It's good to see you whole."

Toby didn't say he'd never be whole, like he would have not long ago. Because he wasn't sure it was true anymore. "I'm sorry for worrying you."

His grandfather pulled back. "We love you. You know that, right?"

"I do. And I know the fae you're mostly meaning are Tia and Mom."

One corner of his mouth lifted. "Well, you are their favorite fae in all the worlds."

"And if I didn't also know Griffin was keeping them updated on every breath I took, I'd make the trip home to check in."

Griffin shifted. "I'm not ... okay, fine. I have the book. Your mother and Tia just worry."

Brandon shared a smile with Toby. "Your mother and sister will survive. It's all Tia can do not to march her entire army here to help you. That's why she wanted me to come."

That surprised him. Tia was on board with this? No wonder Grandfather was so easy to convince.

"Before we continue ..." His grandfather met Toby's gaze. "We must be clear on something. I am here to help protect those like us in this realm. Aghadoon will not be used to hurt humans."

Toby nodded. "If we could do any of this without hurting the humans, you know we would. I promise, we only need a ride. But ..." Grandfather wasn't going to like this. "They need to be able to see it. You know the secrets of Aghadoon better than anyone, can you make that happen?"

He sighed. "Are you certain it has to come to that?"

"The humans know everything now, Grandfather. It's time to make a statement."

With a nod, Brandon closed his eyes and muttered a series of Fargelsian words. Without magic, Toby had never learned the language of his Fargelsian heritage. Not like his mother or Tia. Still, he understood what his grandfather was doing. They weren't words to cast a spell. Instead, they lifted one.

The streets of Aghadoon appeared before them, stretching into the trees that now seemed to have moved.

Those surrounding them talked loudly in confusion.

Brandon lifted his voice. "We will explain everything. For now, you may enter Aghadoon. We will meet in the library at the center of the village." He turned to lead them through the pillars with Griffin at his side.

Xavier didn't move, and Toby stayed with him.

"How is any of this possible?" Xavier shook his head.

"You'd be amazed what's truly possible."

Xavier turned to look at him. "I used to think I knew myself, my heritage, but the fae communities in this world just barely scrape the surface. It's a little terrifying."

"Not for you." Toby hesitated for a moment before boldness struck him and he slid his hand into Xavier's, squeezing. "You never need to fear me or what those I know can do. The ones who should be scared are the humans trying to extinguish us in this world."

"Us?" Xavier gently pulled his hand free. "But you're not one of us, Toby. You come from another world, one we can't even imagine. My father was full-fae, but he was born of this world. His power was strong—for one of us. My mother is human. I have magic but it pales in comparison to this." His gaze lingered on the village. "The humans attacking us are the ones I've lived alongside my entire life."

"No matter the world I call home, I'm here now. I've been to war before. Wars I didn't choose, where too much was placed on my young shoulders. I've been kidnapped by evil kings, forced to help my sister wield untold amounts of power. But this time, I choose to be here. Don't fear me." He lowered his voice. "I don't have the abilities of most of my family, but even if I did, I would never hurt this world. I'd never hurt you. Please believe me."

"I do, Toby." He sighed. "And I know we can't win this without you and the ..." he gestured at the village, "things available to you. I'm just scared that at the end of all this, when you go home, we'll lose anything we've gained."

Toby didn't say it, but he didn't plan to leave until he was sure the fae here would be okay.

They joined the others in the library, where Brandon explained Aghadoon, leaving out the more important facts like what that library held and how the village could travel from place to place as needed. They laid out a plan, and by the time they walked outside, the rain had stopped.

A thumping sounded in the distance, coming from the sky. And then, chatter outside the pillars grew louder by the moment.

"Oh no." Xavier ran down the cobblestone street toward the pillars. He stopped at the entrance and Toby skidded to a halt beside him.

"Who is that?" Toby asked. Large vehicles were parked in the nearby gravel lot. A giant metal bird flew overhead, and Toby ducked with a curse. But it was higher up than he'd thought.

People rushed across the field, carrying all sorts of technology Toby didn't recognize.

These weren't half-fae. They weren't the humans who had risked everything to help them. There was too much eagerness in the air, too much hunger.

"News crews." Xavier peered up at the metal bird with its spinning blades. "This isn't good, Toby. We aren't ready for this."

When he'd asked his grandfather to make the village visible, he hadn't considered the humans would react so quickly.

Xavier was right. They weren't ready for this. "Everyone inside the village. Now!" Toby started running for the village square. "We're leaving for L.A. sooner than we thought!"

Chapter Eleven
SOPHIE-ANN

The stuff the fae read about humans was ridiculous. Also, not entirely untrue. Sophie lay on her stomach, chin propped on one hand as she engrossed herself in yet another human tale. This one bore a striking resemblance to roman gladiator history. Though, all from a fae perspective, of course.

The story was told with a bit of a sneer; Sophie could practically hear the disparaging tone in the way the words were written. Humans killing each other for the entertainment of humans.

"What are you reading?" Tia edged into the room, her strawberry blond hair appearing golden in the sunlight streaming through the arched windows. She could be a queen straight out of a fairy tale, with all her determination and strength.

"Oh." Sophie's face heated. She didn't want to trust any of the fae. Didn't want to believe they could be different than her father had always told her. Evil. But then, she spent the last two days reading all about how the fae saw humans. Blood-thirsty, cruel. They thought humans were the aggressors. "Just something I found in the library."

Tia's face lit up, as if someone held a glow stick underneath her skin. "You found the library?" She hopped onto the bed, having no care that it wrinkled her elegant ruby dress. "It's my favorite place in the palace. We all used to spend the coldest days there, reading all the books my dad didn't want me reading."

"Um, like ... the spicy stuff?" Sophie flushed. Somehow, she couldn't see the feisty queen diving into a romance book.

"Spicy?" Tia tilted her head like she didn't understand the question. "No, but Dad always wanted me reading all the boring books on politics and governing. You know, the stuff he thought I needed to know to be queen." She laughed. "I used to get the biggest book on Iskaltian history I could find and use it as a shield to hide that I was really reading the graphic novels and comic books Uncle Griff used to bring us."

"Your father is ..." Sophie wasn't quite sure how to describe the intimidating Lochlan O'Shea.

"Intense? Definitely. Frustrating? Absolutely. But I'll tell you a secret." She leaned in closer. "He's really a big teddy bear."

Tia loved her father. There was affection in her voice, and one corner of her mouth lifted into a small smile. Whatever Lochlan might be, his daughter idolized him.

They're nothing more than barbarians, Sophie. Her own father's voice echoed in her mind.

But were they? The fae she'd met had connections with other fae not unlike the humans formed. They cared for each other, for their kingdoms and their world. There might not be electricity and little technology, but it wasn't because they couldn't develop it.

There was no need. Magic was their technology.

Tia slid the book out from in front of Sophie. "Oh, this one." Her face darkened. "My Uncle Myles used to tell me all sorts of stories he called human history. There was a time I thought we were so above humans because that kind of thing didn't happen here."

Sophie sensed Tia wasn't done and remained quiet.

"And then, I went to Myrkur." She closed her eyes. "It was a prison realm at the time. Fae fighting fae just to survive. It was horrible." She shivered.

Without thinking, Sophie put a hand on the queen's arm. "I don't think evil has a preference between the worlds."

Tia gave her a tight smile. "You wouldn't have said that when you first crossed the portal."

Wouldn't she? Sophie wanted to believe she hadn't painted an entire species with the same bigoted brush her father had, but maybe that didn't matter. What did was that she hadn't tried to stop him. She'd never told him how wrong it was.

The fae couldn't be trusted. They had magic, and magic was unpredictable. She still believed there was no place for them in her world. But it didn't mean they were evil. She pulled her hand back and used it to push herself up so she was seated next to Tia.

"Why are you here?" Sophie asked.

Tia sighed. "Because I love Gulliver."

Sophie blushed furiously. "I don't need to know that, your Majesty. I ... we never ..." Then, she burst out, "But you're married!"

Tia stared at her for a long moment before doubling over in laughter. "Sometimes, I forget how gloriously obtuse humans can be." She clutched her stomach. "Me? In love with *Gulliver*? Are you mad, human?" She wiped tears from her eyes.

Fury wound through Sophie. What was so funny about it? Was Tia embarrassed by her friend? How dare she laugh about that? "You ..." She couldn't get the words out past her anger.

Tia sobered when she caught sight of Sophie's face. "Oh ... oh no. Sophie, you have to understand. Gulliver is the best man I have ever known. That includes my husband, and Keir is very well aware of this fact. He even agrees. Our friend is kind and brave. Few give him the chance to show who he truly is without prior judgment, and it breaks my heart. But as wonderful as Gullie is, he is part of me. As close as my own brother. Family. That is why I laughed. You'd get the same reaction out of him, you know."

The rage abated, but tendrils of it sat unsettled in her stomach. She wanted nothing to do with Gulliver, yet the thought of another disparaging him, writing him off ... it hurt.

Tia, collecting herself, drew in a breath. "Anyway, as you humans say. I love Gulliver. That's why I'm here. You have to understand something about him. He has spent most of his life looking for the few fae who'd accept him. Sometimes, I fear he doesn't even accept himself. And you ... you're not helping."

"What do you mean?"

"You want to show us that you aren't your father?"

Sophie nodded.

Tia fixed her with a stern look. "Then, start with Gulliver. Trust him. I promise you won't regret it."

Whether she'd regret it or not, Sophie wanted to do as Tia asked. More than anything. She just wasn't sure if she could.

A knock sounded on the door.

"Enter," Tia called.

A young man in castle livery pushed into the room and bowed. "Your Majesty, I've been sent to warn you that your uncle has returned."

"Warn?" Sophie asked.

Tia's lips twitched. "Probably my husband's exact words. Griff tends to cause trouble."

"I thought he helped you?"

"Oh, he does. But I prefer it when he causes trouble for other fae." Tia jumped to her feet with surprising agility in the puffy dress. There was a grace to her, that of an athlete. From a few of the stories Sophie had read about the famed, Tia when she was just a beloved young princess, she knew it was the movements of a warrior.

Tia didn't ask Sophie to stay back, so, out of curiosity, she followed the queen. They found King Keir in the throne room with Gulliver, Griffin, and Brea. All four of them had their voices raised in argument.

No one noticed the arrival of the two women.

Griffin carried a bag that looked very much like an oversized purse on one shoulder. His lips pressed together as his eyes found Tia. "About time, little queen."

Tia grimaced at the title. "And what is your place in this kingdom? Oh, right. You don't have one, uncle."

Griff flashed her a smile. "If that's the case, I'll just return home to my wife. She's the only one I actually enjoy arguing with besides your mother."

"What have you done?" Tia sighed.

Sophie leaned against the wall, hoping no one else noticed her watching them. She eyed Gulliver, the way he seemed to hang on every word his father said. It was just like Tia's love for Lochlan. Sophie couldn't help wondering if that could have been her relationship with her own father had he never joined HAFS.

It was an old organization, one that had its hands in so many things over the years. But it wasn't until her father took over the New Orleans sector that it changed so many lives in her city.

She feared her father, feared for him. And yes, she loved him. But respect? Had there ever been that between them? The kind of trust she saw here just didn't exist in her life.

Griffin pushed a hand through his wily red hair. "It wasn't me this time."

"Is Toby okay?" Brea asked.

"He's fine, Brea."

"But is he safe?" she demanded.

"For now." Griffin nodded.

"I'm starting to think there isn't a safe place anywhere for us in the human realm. You have to convince him to come home."

There was something Griffin didn't want to tell the queen's mother. Sophie could see it in the way he wouldn't look at her.

"Uncle Griff." Tia gripped his arm. "Just tell her."

"He's in Aghadoon ... just outside a human city."

A round of curses issued from Keir and Brea. Sophie watched Brea's face morph from fear to anger and back to fear. But Sophie didn't understand what this Aghadoon was or why it mattered.

"I'm going to murder my father." Brea paced the length of the room. "How could he involve that village in human affairs?" She whirled around to face her daughter. "Did you know about this?"

Tia nodded. Moving to stand beside her husband. "I gave

the order." She tilted her chin up, a powerful queen standing up to the woman who raised her.

"But it's not just human affairs, is it, Brea?" Griffin turned toward her, a softness in his eyes he didn't hold for anyone else in the room. "They're killing fae. Our fae."

"They've been killing fae in the human realm for longer than we know." Tia's shoulders dropped. "It's time we put an end to it, but we cannot start a war."

Brea ran a hand through her dark hair, a deep sigh seemed to deflate her like a balloon as she locked her gaze with Sophie's. "I don't think you fracking fae will ever understand how truly terrifying magic is to humans."

Some of the tension left Sophie's shoulders. Maybe the former queen really did understand what it was like for her to wake up in this world of magic and fantasy come to life.

"I just hope my father has enough sense to keep that village hidden."

"There's a city in the human realm," Griffin said. "I think it's called Lost Angels."

Brea stopped moving. "You mean Los Angeles? I wanted to go there as a kid, but my human parents weren't exactly the family vacation type."

"Yes." Griffin waved away her correction. "It's full of those with fae blood. There are more of them than we could possibly imagine. Thousands just in that one city."

"Thousands?" Confused murmurs erupted around the room. Keir and Tia shared a look of alarm.

"Yes, and I'm afraid we're only at the beginning of what's to come." He dug into the bag on his shoulder and pulled out a folded newspaper, handing it to Tia. "They've done it."

"Done what?" Brea took the paper, opening it so she and Tia could read.

"Oh my," Tia whispered, covering her mouth.

"What?" Gulliver looked confused and slightly scared.

His father met his gaze. "Apparently, we've been outed to their whole world. We aren't just a HAFS conspiracy theory anymore. Human news shows, these odd papers, their governments ... the people now know about us. And they believe it."

Silence followed his words. Sophie could hardly breathe. She'd never imagined her father would do it. Revealing this secret to the wider public meant taking the battle to the next level. He was really going to war.

"So," Keir started, "this piece of paper told you that?"

Brea shook her head. "It tells us that Sophie-Ann Devereaux has been abducted by the fae." She held up the page to show a giant image of Sophie, looking as sick as she ever had.

"I ..." Sophie's eyes widened as she caught the headlines of the *Washington Post*. Her picture took up most of the front page above the fold. Her hand went to her mouth in shock.

HAFS leader's daughter abducted from her death bed by the fae living among us.
An exclusive interview with Claude Devereaux.

"No." She shook her head. But the paper wasn't wrong. The fae abducted her, but it was to save her life. "I'm sorry." It was all she could think to say after her father destroyed any freedom these people had in her world.

Tia snatched the paper, her eyes widening. "We should create one of these news pamphlets. I've seen these many times. The humans get great benefit from it. Our scribes could get to work on it. This is so cool."

"Tia," Gulliver snapped, not taking his eyes from Sophie. "Focus."

"Right, sorry."

Gulliver walked toward Sophie, and she searched for an escape, a place where she could disappear. Surely a magical palace could offer her that.

Her father had always worked so hard to keep her illness a private thing between them. She'd never wanted other people to know and he'd done what he could to protect her from prying eyes. Now, an image of her with a breathing tube and feeding tube was out there for everyone to see. And he was giving interviews with the famous news outlets? It didn't make sense.

Unless ... he wasn't calling the shots anymore.

The story was in the *Washington Post*, which could only mean one thing. This wasn't coming from the New Orleans sector of HAFS bombing single buildings to drive out the fae. They'd connected with the other chapters of HAFS. As far as she knew, they had large groups in all the major cities across the country, probably other countries as well.

If they all came together, and they had the backing of the mainstream news, the fae stood no chance. Not alone.

"Sophie." Gulliver's voice was so soft, so understanding. Yet, she couldn't look at him without seeing the devastation coming for those like him in her world.

"I'm not feeling so well." Sophie ducked around him, running for the exit. She didn't draw a breath until she reached the empty hallway outside. A door opened, and she sprinted past it, not wanting whatever servant it was to witness the tears streaming down her face.

She slammed the door behind her after entering her room and flopped down on the bed.

"Mom," she whispered through her tears, "I don't know what to do."

Her mom was dead because of the fae, because of their

connection to the human world. Yet, she knew her mom would never blame them. She'd always seen the good in everything, everyone.

When had Sophie forgotten that? For so long, she'd let her father's anger and fear poison her.

"Tell me how to help, Mom." Help her father. Help create peace. She didn't want to lose anyone to a war that made no sense.

She buried her face in a pillow, and it grew damp beneath her cheek. But her tears didn't wash away the doubt nor loosen the knot pulling tighter within her.

Chapter Twelve
GULLIVER

"What are you still doing here?" Tia turned on Gulliver like a dragon from one of the human tales who suddenly found a knight trying to steal their gold. Her eyes blazed with the heat of her magic.

Gulliver's brow creased. "Uh ... standing."

Thankfully, Griff came to his defense. "Leave Gulliver alone, Tia." He draped an arm across his son's shoulders. "He's not the reason you're upset right now."

She stomped toward them. "Are you serious?"

"Tia." Keir reached for her, but she swerved out of his reach. "Don't take your frustration out on us. We're on your side. Let's figure out how to help the fae in the human realm without starting a war."

Tia rubbed her eyes. "I'm surrounded by idiots," she murmured.

Brea stepped up to her side, leaning over to whisper. Though, it was loud enough for them all to hear. "They're men. They don't even know what they don't know."

Gulliver looked from one woman to the next, trying to figure out what they could possibly mean. In his opinion, Tia's dad was one of the smartest men in Iskalt. He'd been the one to realize Tia was meant to be queen.

The two women continued to chat in low voices before Keir let out a sound that was half-growl and half-sigh. "Would you care to inform us of our deficiencies?"

Tia's jaw tensed, and her eyes landed on Gulliver. "That girl, the human you so carelessly brought into this mess, is now both the problem and the solution."

"How?" He didn't see how Sophie could do anything about the current issues.

Tia pressed her lips together, studying him before continuing. "First, I must point out that she didn't choose this. You chose it for her."

"She was going to die."

"Yes, I know. But that doesn't change the fact that you and Griff made her a pawn in her father's schemes. He is using her supposed abduction—"

"Not supposed," Griffin interrupted. "We actually did abduct her."

"Quiet. Anyone who is not a queen does not have the right to speak at present." She clasped her hands behind her back, the friendly, goofy Tia falling away. In her place was every bit of the ice queen she'd shown herself to be. "Don't you see? Sophie is further proof we exist. When she goes home and she's seen by the humans, healthy and alive, they will know without a doubt that this drivel is, in fact, not drivel at all." She took the paper and shook it. "We can't undo this unless we keep her here against her will and I'm not prepared to do that. She has to go home to her people. And when she does this will all escalate. Yet, Sophie is also our only connection to the human fighters."

"I don't—"

Tia shut him up with a look. "When I asked what you were still doing here, it's because I expect you to fix your mess. I'm starting to like that woman, and I'm not unhappy that she is alive, but it has created a not-so-small problem for us, and you must do everything in your power to make sure she is on our side."

"Tia ..." Gullie paused. "Am I allowed to speak?"

She nodded.

"Don't think for one second I'm unaware of what I've done, of the risk I have added to our lives. But Sophie ... she's not just a player in your games. You're right that I took her choice away before. I won't do it again. I won't use her. I know you worry for Toby, and I do too. I would lay down my life for him in a heartbeat. You know that. Yet, I will not ask her to do the same. I'm sorry." He turned, hoping she'd call him back, and at the same time hoping she wouldn't.

There had never been anyone in his life he trusted more than Tia, except maybe Griff. They were his people. But this wasn't about trust. At least, not between them. He needed someone else to trust him now.

His feet knew where to take him before his mind caught up, and he found himself standing outside Sophie's door. A maid scurried past, dipping into a curtsy at the sight of him, but he focused on the door, wondering if she'd finally speak to him.

Lifting a hand, he knocked softly against the image of the carved wolf. And waited. There was no answer, and he almost knocked again but thought better of it. If she didn't want to speak with him, he wouldn't force her.

But he hoped she would listen.

His own door was only feet away, and when he entered the room, he walked straight to the far wall, the one he shared with Sophie. The same wall he yelled through to his sisters when they stayed and he needed them to go to sleep or just be quiet and let him sleep.

Inevitably, that alerted them to the fact he was awake, and they'd show up to crawl in bed with him moments later. Their wings constantly got in the way, and they hogged all the covers, but after living his earliest years with little family, he'd never have given it up.

Did Sophie have anyone like that? While he'd observed her in New Orleans, he hadn't seen anyone who appeared to care about her. Sure, she had her father, but did he ever hug her? Did he tell her he was proud of her for fighting so hard to defeat her illness?

Would he have broken someone out of a human healer's ward and taken them through a portal to keep them alive, just because she asked?

The truth was, no matter the hardship in his early life, Gulliver was lucky to have Griffin, Riona, and his sisters.

He just needed Sophie to know she wasn't alone.

Pressing his back to the wall, he slid down until his butt hit the stone floor. A chill raced through him, and he wished he was closer to the hearth, or at least the rug that surrounded the bed.

He pushed his discomfort aside and leaned his head against the wall, gathering every ounce of courage and compassion he possessed. "Sophie-Ann?" His voice was soft, but he knew this room enough to know it reached the person on the other side of that wall.

Still, she didn't respond.

He drew in a deep breath, closing his eyes and focusing on the beating of his heart.

"I was twelve years old the first time I thought I was going to die." He wasn't sure why this story came to mind or what any of it meant in regard to their current problems. "I got trapped in a fortress in Myrkur that was owned by a favorite lord of the king's. This lord liked to keep us in line by withholding food, forcing us into destitution. I lost my parents when I was too young to remember them, but Griffin had looked out for me since the day he set foot in the prison realm. That was what Myrkur used to be. A desolate place of perpetual darkness and never enough resources to go around."

He could see it now. Kavek's giant walls, the river that ran right under them, and the village protecting them from the desperate. But Gulliver never thought about the risks, not then. "I'd thought myself brave, but that's the thing about desperate fae. We will do anything, risk anything, for some kind of hope. I'd never had much of that in my life, not until that night when Griffin showed me the one thing I needed to know."

He paused, taking a breath as images flashed through his mind.

"What was that?" Sophie's voice was low and sweet, curious.

Warmth spread through Gulliver, a kind of precious victory. Not the type one gained in a game, but the kind that was earned and protected. "What was what?"

"The thing you needed to know?"

He touched the wall, imagining she did the same. "He was the first to show me I wasn't alone. That as long as he was there, I'd never be alone again." He pictured her sitting nearby, her pose mirroring his, her heart pounding just as heavily in her chest. "Sophie," he whispered before realizing she probably hadn't heard that. "I didn't bring you here because of who your father is."

When she didn't respond, he continued. "I didn't even

know you were my mission's daughter when we met in that cafe."

"Your mission." She sighed.

That hadn't been the right thing to say. "I liked you. A lot. When I learned you were dying, I wanted to help you. Not so we'd have access to Claude Devereaux's daughter, not even so you'd stay in my life. It was that same hope Griff once gave me ... I wanted you to have it too. I just thought ... you deserved a chance. You deserved to see both worlds for the magical places they are. Whether or not I got to be there when you did, I just needed to know you would have that chance."

Gullie leaned forward against his knees, clasping his hands together as he tried to get the rest out. "But I'm sorry." His voice wavered. "Tia is right. I took the choice away from you. Now, you're in this. All over the human news, in their minds. I know all of this is beyond anything you'd have wanted, but as sorry as I am for the way it happened, I wouldn't take any of it back, not if that meant losing you."

"Gullie." One word. That was all he got.

"I can keep going. You don't need to respond, to accept my apology or forgive me. I know that you will most likely hate me for the rest of your hopefully long life. It's something I will live with. But you need to know, Sophie, that I liked you. Not for my mission. Not because you were sick and needed help. I liked you with your clumsy hands dropping plates of beignets, that tentative smile you have when you think no one is looking and you aren't sure if life deserves a smile. I liked your kindness, and your pretty blue hair. And I liked how you saw me. Even if none of it was real because my fae features were hidden, I enjoyed how you looked at me like I was good and right. Not an abomination."

His tail curled up his spine, the tip thumping in agitation. It didn't like the feeling of being an abomination either.

"In your eyes, I was just like everyone else."

He fell into silence, wishing he could take every word back and knowing he'd done all he could to make Sophie see what she could be. A force for peace. Even if he hadn't said it outright, hadn't asked for it, it was in those words. There was a way for fae and humans to understand each other.

"Sophie." He brushed the wall with his tail. "Please. Say something." Anything.

The quiet stretched for so long that his back ached from sitting on the floor. He didn't know how much time had passed by the time he finally decided to stand and prepare for bed. Nearby, the moon rose outside his window, casting the dark shadows away. In Iskalt, this was when their magic rose, when the power was at its strongest.

For Gullie, life without active power meant having one more thing that placed him on the outside in Iskalt.

He'd given up on hearing from Sophie again and had just removed his shirt when her voice reached him.

"Gullie," she said.

He reached the wall in two long strides and set a palm to it, waiting.

"You were never like everyone else."

And for once, he believed that wasn't such a bad thing after all.

Chapter Thirteen
SOPHIE-ANN

Sophie curled up on a window seat in a remote corner of the library she couldn't get enough of. Bright sunlight illuminated the stained-glass window depicting some long-forgotten queen of Iskalt. It was a strangely warm place, as if some magical force had created the optimal reading nook with the most comfortable cushions and perfect lighting.

The human tale book sat propped against her knees as she studied the fantastical drawings of what fae thought human cities looked like. She'd laughed out loud so many times her sides ached. Instead of steel skyscrapers, the fae illustrator had drawn enormously tall, slender, tent-like structures with stairs wrapping around the outside. It reminded Sophie of a kid's book. Instead of cars, there were carts sitting on streets with nothing to pull them, and men and women walked along sidewalks in the most ridiculous outfits Sophie had ever seen. People wore jeans with long skirts and shirts with ties or plumed hats with hooded sweaters and what looked to be bloomers. Some wore modern sneakers and others wore fashionable shoes from centuries ago.

She'd looked for a copyright page, but there wasn't one. Only a single title page with the year it was crafted. The book was only thirty years old. Sophie didn't know why, but that just made it even funnier.

This book wasn't like the others she'd read. It wasn't a work of fiction so much as an encyclopedia of everything the fae knew about humans, which was next to nothing. As she read about how human technology was their special kind of magic and speculations on how computers worked, she realized there was something innocent and child-like about the fae imagination.

She gazed out the stained-glass window at the snow fields, distorted by the colored glass. It was kind of like the way the fae and humans looked at each other through the invisible barriers that separated them. They were so vastly different in so many ways that it was difficult for one person to understand the other. Yet, in all the ways that truly mattered, weren't they the same?

Sophie snapped the book closed and sat up. She didn't know Tia very well, but the young woman was Queen of Iskalt and well respected among the other nobles from what Sophie had gathered. The queen was cheerful and friendly, with a very strange sense of humor. But there were a few things Sophie knew for certain about Queen Tierney. She loved her family and her people, and she only wanted what was best for them. She also respected humans and their differences. She was loyal, and she wanted to avoid an outright war with the humans.

None of those things were evil qualities, though Sophie had no qualms that the powerful woman was a force to be reckoned with when pushed too far. The idea of Tia's magic scared the wits out of Sophie.

"But can I trust her?" She chewed on her bottom lip. Matters at home were escalating quickly if the news media was talking about fae in any serious tones. That she had somehow become the face of HAFS across the United States was alarming. The outlandish claims her father had made about her ... abduction couldn't continue.

She had to get home. As soon as possible. Before things escalated beyond the point of no return.

Tossing the book aside, Sophie went in search of the queen.

"Now, there's a sentence I never imagined would cross my mind." She pulled the heavy woolen wrap around her shoulders in the drafty halls. She was quickly learning her way around the palace, and the fae were all too eager to point her in the right direction.

Sophie found Tia in a spacious courtyard just outside a study that looked as though a paper factory had exploded across the gilt-edged desk. The queen stood at the center of the circular courtyard, beautiful gray and white plumed birds surrounding her as she fed them bits of bread from her hand.

"They're cute." Sophie approached slowly. The fat little birds waddled like penguins around the queen, searching for discarded crumbs they might have missed.

"They're like greedy little chickens." Tia wiped her hand on her pearl-gray dress.

"They seem to adore you."

"Don't you have snowbirds where you come from?" Tia asked.

"Not like these little guys. They look like a cross between a pigeon and a penguin."

Tierney laughed. "I think you're right." She shooed the

fluffy birds away, moving to sit on a wrought-iron bench and patting the seat beside her.

Sophie joined her, tucking the wide skirts of her dress around her legs before she sat.

"If only we could wear jeans and hoodies." Tia gave a longing sigh.

"Your dresses are so pretty, though."

"Pretty, yes. Comfortable, not in the slightest, but my fae expect their queen to look like a queen, though my mother did set a precedent for casual Friday." Tia laughed again. "Humans definitely have superior comfortable clothing."

"I can't disagree with you there."

The snowbirds had waddled their way back toward the bench, and Tia pulled out a handful of breadcrumbs, flinging them on the snow-covered courtyard. "We need a plan, don't we?"

"We?" Sophie looked up at her in surprise.

"Yes, we. I'm responsible for my fae. Since I was the one who sent Gullie and Toby on a reconnaissance mission to find out what was happening in your world, it's kind of my responsibility to fix it. And your face is all over the human news, so you're as big a part of this as I am."

"You need to send me home," Sophie blurted. "As soon as possible."

Tia nodded. "And what will you do when you get there?"

"My father and his people need to see I'm alive and that I've been healed and returned to them whole."

"And then what?" Tia asked. "Won't that just add fuel to the fire?"

"Well, maybe ... but maybe the violence will stop once they see the fae are not our enemy."

"Is that all it will take?" The queen gave her a skeptical look.

"I need to speak to my father." Sophie sighed. "He will listen to reason. He isn't the only man in charge of HAFS, but his voice holds weight. I will show him I was not abducted against my will, even though that is exactly what Gullie did."

"His heart was in the right place." Tia's mouth curved into a smile.

"I would like to have seen how he and his father managed to get into the hospital without causing a scene."

"Oh, I'm certain they caused trouble somewhere along the way." Tia laughed, and Sophie couldn't get the vision of Gulliver and Griffin attempting to break her out of the ICU out of her mind.

But her smile quickly faded. "HAFS isn't only killing fae. They're killing humans too in their attempt to flush out those with magic. I don't disagree with their mission. Magic has no place in my world, but I can't condone that kind of violence against any people."

"Can you tell me why humans fear us so much?" Tia asked softly. "The ones who believe we exist."

"Like your mother said, magic ... is a terrifying thought for most of us." Sophie fumbled with the soft edges of her wrap, unable to meet Tia's steady gaze. "That an entire race of magical beings walks among us with the power to destroy us at their fingertips isn't something most humans can just accept and move on with their lives."

"To my knowledge, our magic has never been turned against humans in any significant manner. There must be a way we can coexist peacefully."

Sophie's jaw dropped, and her hands curled into fists. "No significant way?" Her words came out in a harsh rasp as anger coiled in her belly. "What about the months of darkness we experienced? Magic was behind that disaster."

Tia blinked at her in confusion. "I'm sure it must have been alarming, but a little darkness never hurt anyone."

"Our world went dark overnight, Tia." She clutched her fists to her side. "We just woke up one morning, and the sun didn't shine. It was there in the sky like always, we could see it, but the darkness of your world choked out the light and chased away the warmth." Angry tears burned Sophie's eyes, and she struggled to keep her composure. "Of course it was terrifying. We had no idea what was happening. Do you even know how close we came to losing everything? Our society was crumbling before our eyes, crime rates soared, and people thought it was the end of the world. That our sun was dying. Our farms were failing because there wasn't enough sunlight for them to grow. People quit their jobs to be with their families, and stores closed. The supply chain broke down, and there wasn't enough food or essentials no matter how much money you had. It was anarchy. Families were starving, and people were dying, Tia. My mother died because of fae magic."

"I see." Tia's hands lay clasped in her lap. "I suppose I never thought about what that must have been like for the human world. I was very young then. But it was mine and my mother's magic that ended the darkness in your world. I guess we were so focused on fixing it and ending the battle against the Dark Fae king that when all was righted and King Egan was defeated ... we went back to our lives."

"In many ways, humans are still trying to get their lives back," Sophie said. "So many humans are struggling to find jobs now. We are still hurting, Tia. From an event that had nothing to do with us. My mother died during the worst time of my life, and I still don't understand why any of it happened."

Tia turned toward her, catching her gaze in that queenly

way she had. "I won't lie to you, Sophie. The fae have a dark history of wars and death. My ancestors have done some really terrible things I am too ashamed to tell you about. During the darkness that invaded your world, we were at war with a very bad man who sought the kind of power no individual should ever have. But we stopped him.

"And now, the five kingdoms have reached a place where we are done looking back on past wrongs. We are finally at peace and striving to do better as we move forward. I want the same things for your people."

"How can we fix this?" Sophie wanted to trust that Tia would make things better for everyone. She just couldn't see how that was possible now.

"I'm so glad you said 'we'." Tia smiled. "We're going to start by sending you home." She gripped Sophie's hand in hers. "But if I do, can I trust you? I don't expect you to choose my side over the humans. I expect you to choose the path to peace between our worlds. Can I count on you for that?"

Sophie nodded. "I will do everything I can to facilitate peace, but in my world, I'm not a queen. I'm just a sick girl without much to offer. I can't force them to listen."

"You have more to offer than you think." Tia laughed. "Just ask Gulliver." She elbowed Sophie playfully.

"What's the plan for when I return?" Sophie ignored the flush that bloomed across her cheeks.

"We could take the time to agonize over a plan and put it into motion, but in my experience, plans never work out the way you expect, and more often than not, they go flying right out the window almost immediately." She stood, grabbed Sophie's hand, and pulled her up.

"Then, what's the alternative?"

"Winging it." Tia shrugged. "We're going to make it up as we go, hoping we don't die before we can return your world to the way it was before we messed it up. Come inside my study. I have a magical object I want you to get acquainted with. It's not scary, I promise, but it will give us a way to stay in touch after you've returned to the humans. We don't have cell phones in the five kingdoms, but we have other ways of staying in touch. Think of my little spelled journals as our way of texting each other. Same technology, different execution."

Chapter Fourteen
GULLIVER

Gulliver thundered down the stairs and across the hall, peeking into rooms and searching every hiding spot he'd ever found his father in. The man was better at avoidance than confrontation, and spending so much time in this palace where both Tia and Brea lived meant a lot of the latter.

But there was only one reason he ever hid from his son.

There was something he couldn't tell him.

Over the years, as Griffin relaxed into a calm life of peace, he lost certain skills he'd needed in previous fights. Like the ability to keep a secret from his children. His face was an open book, the magic in his eyes blazing whenever he was trying to hold something back.

So, he hid.

"Dad!" Gulliver called.

A servant carrying two giant candlesticks he was probably taking to be polished nodded toward the library. Why did everyone choose the same place in this enormous castle to hide?

"I know you're in there." Gulliver tried the handle, but he couldn't push the door open. Something was blocking it. "Come on, Dad."

"Go away." His muffled voice came back through the solid wood.

"Absolutely not. Whatever you're keeping from me, you might as well come out and say it. You know it's only a matter of time."

"You won't be able to get in here. I sealed the door with my magic."

Not for the first time, Gulliver experienced the frustration of having no active power. "Well, then, it really is only a matter of time." Griffin's magic would only last until dawn, which was no more than an hour away. With a shrug, Gulliver sat against the wall, making himself comfortable.

The palace never slept. At night, while Iskaltian magic was alive, fae bustled around, using their power in small ways and large. To clean, to cook, to duel. It was a sight to see, but also incredibly annoying for those without Iskaltian blood who preferred to sleep when the moon was high in the sky.

He'd woken up in the middle of the night with the sense that something was wrong. When he checked his father's rooms, they were empty.

"Gulliver," Griffin yelled, "if you don't leave right now, I'm telling your mother."

Gulliver snorted. "Riona is more likely to punish you than me." She'd recognize immediately what he was doing. Griffin wasn't exactly a reader, not like his brother. The library was only a means to an end for him.

"True," Griffin grunted. "Can you just please walk away right now? I'm begging you."

"Begging? Well, now, I really need to know."

A sigh echoed in the hall, and Gulliver looked up to find the door open and his father standing there in a rumpled burgundy linen shirt and brown pants. He wore no shoes, and that right there was the explanation. There was only one person who'd risk Griffin's wrath waking him from bed and not even giving him time to dress.

Gulliver stood to face him. "What has Tia done now?"

"What?" He started walking, looking away to hide the lies revealed so plainly across his face. "Nothing. You should go back to bed, son. There is nothing that concerns you tonight."

Griffin's words might have told Gulliver to leave, but his steps turned in the direction of the throne room. He was leading him there.

"Why are you lying to me?"

"I'm not." He blinked rapidly, clenching his fists at his sides.

Gulliver rubbed his brow. "How in the magic did you ever fool Egan? Or Reagan? You've duped two evil rulers, and now you can't tell a single lie to your son."

Griffin's step faltered. "This isn't the same thing."

"Why not?" He'd seen Griffin fool the most conniving minds, but not in recent years.

"There is a difference between lying to those who mean nothing to a fae and those one cares about." He veered into the throne room, cutting off further conversation.

But he didn't need to say anything else. He'd brought Gulliver right to the answer.

Sophie.

She stood with Tia and Lochlan, the three of them speaking in low voices.

"No." Gulliver's presence stopped them. "This isn't happening."

"Gul." Tia frowned. "I'm not sure what Griff told you, but—"

"Nothing. He told me nothing because you obviously made him keep a secret. From me. Since when do we do that, Tia?"

"Since you wouldn't agree to this."

"You're right. I wouldn't. I don't." His eyes slid to Sophie's. "You're going back. To him." To her father, the man who wanted to exterminate the fae. "I should have known. You'll never see us as anything other than evil."

"I—"

He cut her off. "Have you been hoping for this the entire time? To return home and join the war against us? I'm sorry we're not precious humans, Sophie-Ann, but it doesn't make us worth any less than you."

"That's enough." Tia's glare cut into him. "Gulliver O'Shea, this isn't like you."

"How are you so sure what I'm like anymore?" He hadn't meant to say the words, but he couldn't call them back now.

He expected Tia to respond with her usual vigor. Instead, it was Sophie who stepped toward him. Her eyes never left his, the soft gaze melting the anger inside him.

"I can still see him." She lifted a hand, placing the lightest touch against his cheek. "That guy I met who ate too many beignets." One corner of her mouth lifted. "I'm sorry too, Gullie. I should have said it last night while you poured out your heart through that wall. I'm sorry I spent so much of my life hating those like you. You're a good man." She pulled her hand away. "For a fae."

When she stepped back and turned to Lochlan, all Gullie could do was watch as his uncle opened a portal and blue light flashed through the room. Sophie looked back over her shoulder, giving him a sad smile before stepping through. It was only then Gulliver saw the familiar journal in her hands. She wasn't going back to her father for herself. It was for them.

"No." Gullie recovered enough to run after her, to try to jump into the portal after Lochlan. His feet hit the ground, but when he looked around, the throne room still surrounded him and the portal was gone.

Sophie was gone.

He touched his cheek, still feeling the ghost of her fingers, still not sure what had happened, what was going to happen.

A hand landed on his shoulder. "See, Gul, she doesn't hate you after all."

He ripped himself away from Tia. "You don't get to say that to me."

"Be reasonable. We all knew this was going to happen one way or another."

No, he refused to believe that. They had other options to help the fae in the human realm. There had to be ways that didn't put someone he … cared about in jeopardy. "You talked all about choice, how I took hers away by bringing her here. What about you, your Majesty?" He spit out the title. "You don't think you did exactly the same thing, sending her back into a budding war?"

"No, I don't. There's a difference. I am the queen. It is my job to protect the fae, to make the sacrifices necessary for my kingdom."

"So, she's a sacrifice then? I'm so glad we cleared that up. It's fine for the human I love to become a sacrifice, but your brother joins the war and you do everything in your power to try to get him to come home."

Tia's indignation faded away in an instant, and her shoulders dropped. "Oh, Gullie."

"What?" He didn't like the way she was looking at him. With pity.

"I'd had my suspicions, as you know. But there were doubts too. You really love her, don't you?"

"No. I didn't say that."

Griffin cleared his throat. "Uh, you did, actually."

"No one asked you," Tia and Gulliver said simultaneously. That broke the tension, and they shared a smile.

"Go jump in the frozen lake or something," Tia told Griff, not looking at him.

Gulliver lifted one brow. "Or he could hang out on the balcony in the snow."

"Go to Fargelsi and listen to Myles talk about human movies."

"I get it!" Griffin headed to the door. "I'm leaving so you two can be mean without me."

When he was gone, the silence lasted a few moments before both Gullie and Tia laughed. Their laughter died away, and Tia sighed.

"It was her choice."

Gulliver wanted to say that was a lie, but he felt in his gut it was true. "Is she ..."

"On our side? Not likely."

"And yet, you sent her back to her father?" He would probably never understand Tia.

"She's not not on our side."

"You make no sense."

Tia walked toward her throne and collapsed into it. She patted the lower throne next to her and Gulliver sat. "She's on the side for peace."

Tia picked at the edge of the golden armrest, her gaze

focused on her fingers. "She's for peace, but Sophie doesn't fully trust us. Like most humans, she sees our power as a threat to her world."

"She's not wrong."

Tia sighed. "No, she's not. But I think she sees us differently now. We aren't the barbaric creatures she'd been told we were, animals who wanted to destroy everything she loved. She thinks her return can bring peace."

"And what do you think?" Gulliver looked at her, waiting for the answer he knew was coming. He'd always been an optimist, thinking with his heart. Tia was the opposite. She expected the worst and was usually right.

"I think we're past the point where peace is possible." She rubbed her eyes, exhaustion evident on her face. "They hate us, Gul. Sophie may have started to change her mind, but the entire human world now knows we exist, that we can come take what they have at any moment."

She was right. If the fae invaded the human world, the humans would stand no chance. The darkness almost destroyed their civilization. What would a sudden onslaught of magic do?

"That's why you haven't wanted to get more involved." It made more sense now. "The half-fae living there have little, if any, power. But if an army from Iskalt suddenly appears, there's no coming back from that."

She nodded. "The humans deserve their world just as much as we deserve ours. I don't want to take it, but if I aided in this war, I'd almost have to. Just to keep our fae safe."

"So, we just sit here and watch those with our blood die?"

She fixed him with a stern look. "I didn't say that, did I?"

"Kind of."

"Gul, Sophie will try to turn her father's opinion, to make

him see war isn't the answer. And that's great, but I have little faith it will work in any significant way."

Gulliver turned on the throne to face her. "You're sending me back in, aren't you?"

She gave him a tiny smile. "There's a reason you're you and I'm me, a reason we're us. You know exactly what I'd do at all times. I need that. Toby is impulsive now, apparently. Brandon is righteous. Griffin is reckless. I need an agent there to keep a cool head, to make sure Toby stays safe and that no one does anything irrevocably stupid."

Tia reached for his hand. "There is no one I trust more than you. If I can't be there myself, it makes me feel better if you are. Please, Gullie, protect our fae. And for the love of magic, keep them from destroying the humans altogether."

Gulliver would never say no to Tia, and this time was no exception. He stood, giving her a nod. A mission like this beat sitting around the palace waiting for news.

"I'll find my father and we'll prepare to leave tomorrow night." He started to leave, but Tia called him back.

"Gul?"

He looked over his shoulder. "Is there something else?"

"Sophie ... she may not want to, but I think she cares about you too."

A smile curved his lips, and his cheeks heated. "Did you see her touch my cheek?" Like he hadn't repulsed her, like she saw him. Nothing had ever felt more real.

Tia laughed. "You're such a nerd."

That was a human word he didn't quite understand, but from the way Tia smiled, he assumed it was a term of endearment, another way to tell him she loved him. "You're a nerd too, Tia."

Chapter Fifteen
TOBY

After a brief stopover in the middle of nowhere to regroup from the onslaught of the human media, Toby and Brandon moved Aghadoon to their newest location. Los Angeles.

Not wanting to cause too much of a stir this time, they'd looked for a more private area. And at first, the small park in L.A. seemed like the perfect location. It was a small green meadow in the foothills, where humans came to walk their dogs and get some exercise and fresh air away from their smoggy city. Some of the people seemed obsessed with having their picture taken in front of a weird sign higher up in the hills.

But that was the first day. Toby hardly recognized Lake Hollywood Park now. Like the first location where his grandfather had settled the tiny village of Aghadoon, the park soon swarmed with news crews and dozens of those metal birds hovered above as more and more humans came to get a glimpse of the fae village that had dropped out of the sky. But they were prepared for it this time.

They weren't a secret anymore, but Toby was one of the few who were okay with it. That was his intention all along when he'd asked his grandfather to make the village visible. It was time for the humans to get used to them being here. The fae would no longer hide in plain sight.

After weeks of living among the very human-like fae of this world, Toby knew better than anyone that this world was their home. He couldn't imagine forcing those like Xavier to move into the fae world and expect them to adapt. He intended to help them fight for the right to stay.

"Such a fuss over one little village." His grandfather stood beside him at the entrance to Aghadoon, watching the scene play out in front of them.

The local fae had flocked to the village the moment their arrival hit the news outlets. Toby had never imagined just how many fae there were in this country. "Well, a magical flying village is a rather strange thing even for us, Grandfather. I think you've just gotten used to the idea of Aghadoon over the years. For the humans and fae of this world, this kind of magic is astounding."

Toby watched the swarm of humans and their special guard force keeping the crowd at bay. No one walked their dogs in the park now. The grassy meadow was empty beyond the borders of Aghadoon, and a wide-open space stood between the human peacekeepers and their fae counterparts. The local fae communities had been quick to form a security force around the park to keep the humans out.

"I thought Aghadoon would be big enough to serve as a haven for the fae in this region." Toby shook his head at the sheer number of fae that had joined them inside the village and those outside protecting it. "I had no idea of their numbers, but clearly Aghadoon is only a start to what we actually need."

"Clearly, that is the least of our worries." Toby's grandfather pointed to the line of humans hidden behind their protectors. They carried signs and chanted.

Say no to fae!

Go back to your own world! This one's ours!

Fight today for a magic-less tomorrow!

Keep your eternal night to yourselves!

End the magic before it ends us!

We will not be victims of magic!

Others were more clearly from HAFS. Their signs and chants amounted to a single message.

Bring Sophie home.

And on and on it went. The hatred they spewed for an entire group of people they didn't even know broke a piece of Toby's heart. But others seemed to be in favor of the fae. They came with smiles and signs welcoming them to L.A. They took pictures of the village and tried to break past the human security forces.

"We have other matters to attend to, Toby." Brandon laid a hand on his grandson's shoulder. Together they turned, leaving the chaos behind. They walked up the ancient path to the library near the center of the village. Others followed, but only select fae were admitted in.

Inside, the library swarmed with activity. Xavier argued with several local leaders of the Los Angeles settlements.

"Your arrival in this manner has blown the lid off the secrecy we have all worked so hard to maintain for centuries." A formidable-looking woman slammed her fist against the worn wooden table at the center of the room. "It was not your choice to make, young man." She stood with her hands on ample hips, glaring at Xavier like she secretly wanted to tear him limb from limb and be done with him.

"It wasn't his choice, ma'am." Toby stepped forward.

She turned on him, eyes smoldering with anger. "And just who are you?"

"Tobias O'Shea, Prince of Iskalt." He gave her a regal nod, standing beside his grandfather with his hands clasped behind his back.

"Prince?" She gaped at him.

"Yes, madame. My sister, the Queen of Iskalt, is concerned over the death of fae in this land. It is our intention to help those who need it."

"You want to help?" She seemed to have gathered her wits about her, and her anger returned. "Perhaps you should return to your world and leave the humans to us. You've caused more damage than you can possibly understand."

"Oh, I understand, Ms. ...?" He trailed off.

"Meara ... er, your Highness. Leader of the Hollywood Hills fae." There were several other leaders among the small group gathered around the table, and they were all mad.

Toby had some work to do to win them over. "I understand perfectly well what we've done, and it's about time someone brought the fae out of the shadows and into the light of day." Toby moved to stand beside Xavier at the head of the table. "This world belongs to you all as much as the humans. You've been here for generations—so long none of you would know what to do with yourselves in the five kingdoms."

Toby pointed toward the park. "They would have you leave. Send you back to a place as foreign to you as the moon is to them. It's not fair. You're here. You have some level of magic the humans don't. So what?"

"So what?" A deadly soft voice rose above the noise from

outside. Toby turned toward the door where a woman had just entered.

"Orla?" Xavier moved toward her. "I'm so glad you could make it. Please come join us."

"For what?" She moved like a warrior, her eyes not missing a single detail of her surroundings. She had magic. Much more than most of the fae Toby had met in the human world. This woman had very little human in her heritage.

"We need to come up with a plan." Toby gestured for everyone to sit.

"Obviously." Orla took the seat at the opposite end of the table from Toby. The one nearest the exit.

"Toby, this is Orla," Xavier announced. "She is the leader of all the fae settlements in the Los Angeles area."

"Excellent." Toby nodded, playing the part of the royal delegate to perfection. "The fae of this world need a haven. A home where they can live openly and peacefully, without fear and without the need to hide their identities."

"You ask for too much, young prince," Meara said. "You are not of this world. You cannot understand what the humans will do to those with magic. You come from a place where magic is an effortless thing. Here, we struggle to maintain what little magic we have. We are not as strong as you are. We cannot protect ourselves from human weapons."

"First and foremost, you should all know that I have no real magic to speak of. Most of you here at this table could out magic me on your worst day. With that in mind, I still believe we can protect our fae in this realm and live peacefully among humans."

"And how do you propose we do that?" Orla leaned back in her seat. Pulling one knee up to her chest, she rested her forearm on her knee. The tips of her pointed ears protruded through her dark hair that hung like a curtain down her back. Her pale golden eyes shot right through Toby.

"For the moment, Aghadoon will serve as a haven for any fae in fear for their lives. But we need to think bigger. There are more fae in this city than there are in the largest cities of the five kingdoms. They need a sanctuary." Toby locked his gaze with Orla's. "And I need your help to protect them."

Orla studied him for a moment before she nodded. "You've pulled us into the fire already, Prince. You'll either save us or get us all killed." She let out a sigh as she gazed at her fellow leaders. "Just promise me one thing."

"If it's within my power to grant."

"If this goes poorly, will you help those who wish to leave this world?"

"Return to the fae world?" Toby asked, and she nodded. "That is the one thing I can guarantee. I will take them home to our world myself."

"Might I also ask a favor, your Highness?" Meara asked.

"You may ask," Toby said in a tone that indicated he might not grant her request.

"None of us knows one kingdom from five. Can someone here help ... educate us on the places of refuge we might seek in your world? Should it come to that."

Toby glanced at his grandfather in silent communication before Brandon gave a slight nod. "Yes," Toby promised. "My grandfather, Prince Brandon, is the authority of Aghadoon. He will see to it that all the pertinent information on the five kingdoms is available to anyone who wishes to learn about their heritage."

"For those with magic, I should be able to help them learn which of the five kingdoms they originally hailed from," Brandon offered. "That might help them make their decision on where to go if they feel they must leave their home here in Los Angeles."

"And should they wish to seek refuge in our world, I will take them where they would like to go," Toby added. "But they must report directly to the king or queen of the land they seek refuge in. I can assure you, each of the rulers of our world is every bit as approachable as myself."

"All right." Orla stood. "What's our next move?"

"We go out there." Toby pointed to the park, where the news crews had gathered. "We go as a united front to speak with your media people. The ones with the vans and the sticks they shove in people's faces."

"The reporters?" Meara chuckled. "You want to go talk to the media?"

"I have something to say that they need to hear."

"This should be good." Orla shook her head and was the first through the door.

"What are you doing?" Xavier walked beside Toby through the streets of Aghadoon.

Toby slowed his pace, letting the others pull ahead of them. Reaching for Xavier's hand, Toby laced his fingers through his. "I need you to trust me."

Xavier met his gaze for a moment and then squeezed his hand before releasing it. "I trust you."

They began walking again in silence. "There's just one thing."

"What?" Xavier's eyes widened at the sight of all the cameras and people swarming the perimeter of the park.

"What's it called here when a person or government designates a region as a sanctuary?"

"We have Sanctuary Cities all across America, but I'm not sure that's what you're getting at. Maybe a City State? Why?"

"Not sure yet." He stepped through the pillars marking the exit from Aghadoon.

"You don't have a plan, do you?" Xavier's voice came out a bit higher than normal.

"As my mother would say, I'm winging it." Toby crossed the grassy expanse.

"Greetings, humans." Toby waved at a group of news people as they approached the line of human protectors. "I have an announcement I'd like you to put on your televisions."

"He's going to get us all killed," Orla muttered under her breath as camera crews broke through the line of security and mobbed their group.

"Who are you?" Someone stuck one of their strange speaking sticks in Toby's face.

"My name is Tobias O'Shea, prince of a land called Iskalt."

"What do you want from us?"

"From humans?" Toby blinked at them. "For my people to be left alone. I wish for humans and fae to coexist peacefully, so I may return to my kingdom with the good news."

"Do you plan to kill all the humans?"

"What? Don't be ridiculous."

"What my friend here is trying to say," Xavier stepped up beside Toby, "is that the fae have been living among you for generations, and we've never intentionally harmed anyone."

"What about the long night?"

"That was a long time ago," Toby said. "It was an accident that my sister and I worked tirelessly to fix. I can assure you that nothing like that will ever happen again." Another reporter tried to interject, but Toby cut him off. "I came here to announce that there will be changes in our future. Necessary changes to ensure the safety of my people. As a Prince of

Iskalt, I claim the city of Los Angeles and its surrounding areas as a City State for the fae living in this world." Xavier turned him toward the nearest camera, urging him to continue as silence fell across the park. The only sound was the clicking of their black, flashing boxes.

"Wherever you are in this world, all fae are welcome in this city. Los Angeles will be a haven. My people will ensure your safety within the borders of our new City State. Together, we will live under our own laws, and we will do so peacefully, right alongside our human friends. You have no need to fear us, but please ..." Toby's voice failed as a wave of sadness swept over him. "Please stop killing us. Any human who wishes to live peacefully among us is welcome to stay in Los Angeles. Those who continue to use violence against us do so at their own peril."

Toby stepped back. "That is all."

Sound returned as suddenly as it had faded as reporters fired questions at him. But Toby said nothing as he led his fae back up to the safety of Aghadoon.

"You know what you've done, don't you?" Orla asked.

"I've staked a claim on this land, so your people will have a place of refuge."

"Maybe. But right now, you've declared open season on all the fae living in this city. None of my people are safe here, so you'd better follow through with your promise to protect them." She reached for his shoulder, pulling him to a stop. "Because if you don't, prince or not, I will kill you myself."

Chapter Sixteen
SOPHIE-ANN

"I only want my daughter back." Sophie listened to her father's voice over the radio as she leaned back on the torn leather seat of the cab taking her to the one place she knew the man would be.

I really hope that's true, Dad.

She'd been in a gas station getting snacks with the little bit of human money Lochlan had given her when she saw Tia's brother on the news. He probably didn't even realize he'd basically declared war on the humans. There was no way the American government would allow the fae to take Los Angeles for their own without a fight.

He'd just made everything worse.

She wasn't sure why she cared so much, or what she was going to do when she faced her father, but part of her just wanted to see the relief on his face when he found out she was alive. She wanted to know he truly cared.

L.A. was the logical place for him to be after Toby's announcement. It would become the staging ground for any further attacks on the fae. Palm trees lined the road, their shadows shielding cars from the harsh California sun. There was a familiarity here, despite the fact it had been years since she accompanied her father to the L.A. HAFS headquarters.

The largest sector of the organization was here in this city filled with fae. Unlike in New Orleans, HAFS wasn't welcome, even by other humans, so they operated under even stricter secrecy.

The cab pulled up in front of a dilapidated building on the outskirts of the city, one that held deception in every chipped cement block, every broken window. After paying the driver, she got out and stared up at the enormous structure. No one came or went through the front entrance. She remembered that, yet she knew the guards would already have caught her on camera.

So, she waited.

There were two of them. They wore plain jeans and polo shirts, no indication that they guarded the heavily fortified building. Both men had tattoos stretching up the pale skin of their arms, a language she couldn't decipher.

Lifting her chin, she met their curious gazes, choosing to ignore the handguns attached to their belts. Neither man moved to pull their weapons.

"This is a secure facility," the first one said, his tone mocking, as if a girl like her couldn't possibly understand.

"Wait." The second one put a hand on his comrade's chest to hold him back. "She look familiar to you?"

"No."

"I swear I've seen—" His eyes widened.

Sophie didn't wait for him to put it together. "I'm Sophie-Ann Devereaux. You will take me to see my father."

Second douche-bag hit the first one's arm. "Luke, we've got her. Imagine the reward. I knew she was alive."

The first, Luke, didn't speak as he stepped forward, reaching for Sophie. A meaty hand landed on her shoulder, sending a spike of pain through her that she tried to ignore. "You're coming with us." He shoved her toward the door, waiting for his friend to open it.

They entered what appeared to be an abandoned warehouse. A blank canvas of broken concrete stretched past fractured wooden chairs and abandoned desks, ending at a set of heavy steel elevator doors. The only indication that this was something other than a symbol of the past was a small keypad by the elevator.

Sophie stumbled forward with a shove from behind. The second guard walked ahead of them, entering five numbers into the keypad and then pressing his thumb to a biometric scanner below. The doors opened silently. No sound of machinery, no creaking of the metal.

It was like the suffocating air drew all noise from the room as Luke pushed her across the threshold. The second guard didn't join them before the doors closed.

By the time they reached the lower level, all manner of noises invaded her senses. Luke's heavy breathing. Chatter coming from the other side of the door. The clacking of keyboards. Somewhere, an alarm sounded before cutting off suddenly.

When the doors opened, Sophie found herself in L.A. HAFS command. Rows and rows of computers filled the large room. Giant screens spanned the back wall, where guards watched videos of various parts of the city.

"Luke," a too-familiar voice called. "Heard you captured an intruder and—" Gabe stopped in front of them, his wide eyes traveling over her face, down the length of her neck. He shook his head, as if he didn't believe what he saw.

"She says she's the Devereaux girl." Luke's hand closed

around her arm in a vice-like grip. "Nick seemed to believe her, but we all know the truth. Whether the old man will admit it or not, his daughter is dead."

"Thanks, Luke." Gabe's jaw tightened. Sophie recognized that look. Since he was a kid, he'd had problems with anger, and he was about to lose control if the other man didn't back off right now. "I'll handle the intruder from here."

Nick's grip tightened. "Like fae you will."

Sophie winced from the pain, and Gabe's eyes darkened. He stepped toward Nick. "You will take your filthy hand off her right this moment, or I will break every one of your fingers as I do it myself."

Indecision warred in Nick's eyes before he released her with a shove toward Gabe. "I don't need the trouble."

"Return to your post."

With a growl, Nick left Sophie standing alone in a sea of people with the man she was supposed to have married. Married and then left as a widower. She'd have been the perfect wife for him when she was dead. Then he could inherit everything her father had created.

Gabe didn't speak for a long moment as he stared at her. His hard eyes softened. Then, in a rush of breath, he said, "How are you here? No, you don't have to answer that. Not to me. Save the answers for your father. Soph, I thought you were dead."

"I'm supposed to be." She rubbed her arm where she was sure she'd have a bruise from the guard's grip. "I'm not."

His lips curled into a smile much kinder than any she'd seen on his face before. "That's good. I'm glad." He looked like he wanted to hug her or kiss her or just anything to prove she was really there.

Sophie reached out, gripping his hand. Whatever he'd

turned into, they'd once been friends. "I have stories, Gabe. They saved me."

His smile fell, and he leaned closer. "If you're talking about who I think you are, don't say that here."

"Sophie-Ann?" Another member of the New Orleans HAFS sector recognized her, her voice way too loud. Others crowded in, some recognizable, some new to her. They repeated her name, like it couldn't possibly be true.

Gabe wrapped an arm around her as he shouted at them to stay back. No one listened to him. The noise became all she heard, the crowd all she saw. She stood frozen to the spot, unable to make any of it stop.

Not until another sweeping voice yelled above the din. "What is going on here?" The familiar admonishment in his voice gave Sophie comfort. Her father had always been a harsh man, but never unfair. Not to her or those who followed him.

He pushed his way through the crowd, coming to a stop when he'd almost reached her. There was no reaction on his face, no relief in his eyes.

Gabe released her, and for once, she wished he'd pull her back against him, protect her from the realities she'd returned to face. Drawing in the courage Gulliver told her she had, she stepped toward her father.

"Hi, Dad." She shrugged one shoulder.

"Soph." He reached out, touching a strand of her hair that had fallen forward in the squeeze of the crowd. It was smoother now, stronger than the wisps of hair left from chemo. The magic had strengthened every part of her.

"Did I miss anything?" Like a war.

As if something snapped inside him, he yanked her into a crushing hug, the kind that stole a child's fears, their doubts.

Sophie let herself sink into him, soak in the safety a father's arms should represent.

"I was so afraid for you," her father whispered.

He'd also used her disappearance to further this war, but now was not the time to bring that up. "I'm okay. I promise."

"But how." He moved her out to arm's length to examine her.

"Maybe we should give my fiancée some space." Gabe led the others away to give her some privacy with her father.

Sophie cringed at the word fiancée. Everything she'd been through finally gave her the courage to do what needed to be done. Turning away from her father, she waited for Gabe to meet her gaze. "Look, I'm going to be honest. I never said yes to marrying you in the first place. I thought I was dying, so I never intended to live as your wife. Now that I'm still here, I still don't plan that. Sorry, Gabe, but the wedding is off."

She expected her father to protest, but instead, he only stared at her. "You're different."

"No, I'm still me. Just the version of myself I never got to be." The version Gullie saw. She shoved thoughts of him to the back of her mind, worried she'd never see him again. "Dad, can we speak alone?"

"That's not a good idea." An unfamiliar man walked toward them, the others giving him a wide berth. He was tall, thin, and wholly intimidating. With gray hair and crystalline eyes, there was an intensity about him.

"Honey." Her dad drew her against his side. "Meet Commander Clarkson, the leader of the worldwide HAFS. He oversees every sector."

Sophie had heard about Doctor Alec Clarkson. His name was spoken of in hushed voices. Even those in HAFS feared him, feared what he could do to them. Rumor was he had a series of institutions across the world, where he locked up those suspected of having magic so he could study them. Now, his eyes were set firmly on her.

"From what I gather, Miss Devereaux, the last time anyone saw you, you were at death's door." A dark, bushy brow rose in question.

Sophie resisted the urge to shrink away from him. "I …" She stood to her full height. "The fae saved my life."

Shocked voices rose around her, some angry, others merely curious.

Commander Clarkson rubbed his ridiculously groomed mustache. "So, you're saying you're one of them now?"

It didn't escape her notice how her father loosened his grip and stepped away from her. That should have hurt, but she'd deal with him later. "No, what I'm saying is that maybe there's more to them than we thought." This was what she'd come back for, what she needed to do.

"She's full of their magic," someone yelled. "You can practically smell it on her." The crowd gave her more and more space until she was an island, separated from anyone else by the angry swells. Even her father drifted from her side, refusing to meet her gaze.

Still, the doctor didn't react. His calm was calculated, dangerous. In him, Sophie recognized a ruthlessness she'd never seen before. This was a man to be careful of.

"No." She tried to raise her voice enough to be heard over the scared and vengeful HAFS members.

"Don't you remember the darkness?"

"They're going to destroy us!"

"They won't." Sophie turned, trying to find whoever said that. "The fae only want to live in peace. They helped me when they didn't have to. I met one of their queens, and they don't want a war."

It was as if none of them could hear her, or maybe they just didn't want to. "Listen to me!" she yelled. "We have to stop this. No more humans or fae have to die." Desperation flooded her as she realized what she'd refused to acknowledge before.

It was too late. These people had gone down a road none of them wanted to come back from. There were no forks, no roundabouts allowing for a quick change in direction. It was a straight line between here and a war that could destroy everything. A war they thirsted for.

Still, Commander Clarkson only watched her.

"I'm sorry, sir." Her father grabbed her arm. "My daughter is obviously still not well. She's confused."

"Dad, I'm—"

He ignored her. "I will take her somewhere to rest from her journey."

Commander Clarkson pinned those intense eyes on her father. "I expect you to deal with this."

He nodded, steering Sophie away from the crowd.

"Dad." She tried to break away from him. "What are you doing? Let me go."

"Not until you're my daughter again." He guided her down a series of hallways, never letting go. Stopping at a heavy steel door, he produced a key and unlocked it, shoving her in. "Sophie, I love you, but right now, you must decide which side you're on. I can't protect you in this. I won't."

Those final words echoed in the nearly empty concrete room long after he locked her in. She sank onto the small cot, burying her face in her hands.

I can't protect you. I won't.

If she wanted to do the right thing, she truly was alone.

Chapter Seventeen
GULLIVER

Gulliver walked across Lake Hollywood Park, lost in the wonderful discovery he'd made just this afternoon. Today would forever be an important day in his life.

The day he discovered tacos.

He'd made the trip down to the street vendor three times since lunch. The first time was an accident. He was supposed to meet a small group of fae refugees who would be staying in Aghadoon. He'd found the tacos on the way. On the trip back, he'd made them wait while he bought more tacos before he finally escorted them into Aghadoon to one of the small houses they'd set aside for the local fae who might be in danger.

A wonderful aroma had caught his attention on that first trip, and a very nice human man with a thick mustache asked him if he'd like a taco. Gulliver didn't know what a taco was, but he knew he needed to taste whatever the man had secreted away inside his restaurant on wheels. And it was the best decision of Gulliver's life.

He'd always loved human food. Cheeseburgers were his favorite, and Chinese dumplings were high on the list too. Pizza was life, but tacos? Pure ecstasy.

He'd never had anything like the crunchy shell of deliciousness filled with meats and cheeses and spicy sauces. It was sort of like the meat pies he loved from home but better. Tacos came in all kinds of flavors. There were even some with soft chewy wraps filled with fried things called shrimp and fluffy white rice and flecks of herbs and spices Gulliver couldn't place. The funny green goo was his favorite—cool, creamy, and tangy with bits of onion and lime. It cut through the heat of some of the spices.

He did not like the crunchy green peppers that made his eyes water.

Biting into his seventh or eighth taco of the afternoon, Gulliver decided he liked the carnitas the best, though he had no idea what a carnita was. Melted cheese and a burst of sour cream hit his tongue, and he groaned out loud.

"So good." He rubbed his belly as he strolled up to the pillar entrance of Aghadoon with a bag full of tacos he intended to share with his dad and maybe Toby too if there was enough, but he was already second-guessing that decision.

"Stop right there." Someone shoved Gulliver back a few paces, and he almost dropped his taco. Good for the buffoon who struck him that he managed to save the last precious few bites. But a dollop of sour cream and the green stuff splattered on the grass at his feet.

"Hey, watch it. That was the best part." Gulliver clutched the bag to his chest to keep them safe.

"What business do you have in Aghadoon?" the fae demanded.

"Business?" Gulliver scowled at the new guard. "No business of yours." He tried to sidestep the guard, but the fae lurched in front of him, a wall of chest and arms keeping him from the entrance.

"What, do you expect me to sleep in the park? I'm full from my lunch. I need a nap, and you're keeping me from it."

"Aghadoon is only open to the fae. Get out of here, boy."

"Boy?" Gulliver lifted his chin, prepared to kick this fae and run. His dark fae features were hidden in this realm, but that didn't make him any less fae.

The fae shoved him again, and Gulliver dropped his bag of tacos. The guard stepped on them, crushing the delicate shells.

"No!" Gulliver gasped. "Okay, *now*, I'm angry." He gathered up the bag, dusting off the bits of dirt and grass. "And don't think I won't eat this. I'm out of funny human money, and I lost Tia's plastic money card."

"Get lost, kid."

"No. I think you owe me three new tacos. Unbroken ones, if you please."

"I owe you a black eye if you don't get lost now."

"I've been lost most of the time I've been in the human realm. I'd like to avoid that if possible."

"Gullie, what's the trouble here?" Griffin came up behind him, whistling a tuneless song.

"This ... fae won't let me in, and I'm late for my afternoon nap." Gulliver thrust a finger into the guard's face. "And he hurt my tacos."

"Well, that's really not a good idea, young sir," Griffin said. "I can personally attest to how cranky my son gets if he misses his nap. Worse than his little sisters. And if you messed with his food, you'll never hear the end of it."

"Don't be rude, Dad. You take naps too."

"I'm old. I have excuses. Old war injuries and the like." Griffin patted his son's shoulder, and Gulliver snorted a laugh.

"Please let us through, and we'll be out of your way." Griffin gave a nod of respect to the guard.

"Get out of here. Both of you." The fae folded huge arms over a barrel chest.

"This one has the look of an ogre about him, doesn't he, Dad?" Gulliver was growing impatient. That last taco was one too many, and he needed a moment in the privy before that nap.

"No need for that tone." Griffin pulled himself up to his full height. "I'm sure you'll find our names on your list there." He pushed hair over the tip of one of his pointed, obviously fae ears.

"Sir! Sir!" One of the humans with a funny-looking stick in her hand waved to get Gulliver's attention.

"Go away." The guard barked at the woman and pointed Gulliver and Griffin back the way they came, completely ignoring Griffin's hints at his non-human heritage.

"Looks like we're going to have to sneak in," Griffin muttered as they retreated. "I don't suppose there's a back way into Aghadoon?"

"Probably, but you'd need magic to find it, and at the moment that counts both of us out." Gulliver stared up into the brilliant sunlight of a beautiful California afternoon. He'd just learned that was where Los Angeles was, in a kingdom called California. It was supposedly near an ocean, where humans liked to swim, but in Gulliver's experience, oceans meant dangerous creatures, violent storms, wicked hot temperatures along the fire plains, or freezing icy blasts along the shores of Iskalt. Humans did the oddest things for entertainment.

"Sir?" The woman waved at them again. "Care to make a statement?" She held her stick out, and Gulliver glanced at his father before they crossed the park to where she stood with the other humans behind a bright yellow stretch of tape that wouldn't keep anyone out if they really wanted to visit the park or the fae village that had landed there.

"Beautiful day we're having," Griffin said in his most endearing voice.

"Are you fae?" She spoke into her stick and then turned it back toward them.

"Yes, we are," Gulliver said warily.

"I am Prince Griffin of Iskalt and keeper of the rift in Myrkur." Griffin sank into a courtly bow. "This is my son, Lord Gulliver of Myrkur."

"Lovely to meet you," the nice lady said, her red lips curving into a friendly smile. "Can you tell us why the fae have come to our world?" She held the black stick in Griffin's face. "So many humans believe you've come to take over. Can you comment on that?"

Griffin laughed, shaking his head as he attempted to charm the young lady. "Just a few short years ago, we only had three kingdoms. Now, after a long war and some magical mishaps that hid part of our world for eons, we're up to five huge kingdoms. And here we are in the human realm now." He shrugged. "Who knows what's next?"

"I'm only here to eat," Gulliver added as the woman grew silent. "Humans make the best food."

"F-food?" she stammered, taking a step back.

"Uncle Griff!" Toby called to them from the entrance to the village. "Gullie, let's go."

"Oh, hey, Tobes." Gulliver walked away from the lady, who didn't seem so interested in talking to them anymore. "You know the new guards wouldn't let us in?"

Toby waved them through the line of local fae working security. "I added your names to the list of approved fae; he should have let you in." Toby led them up to the library at a quick pace. "Others have to answer questions first."

"They didn't even ask our names, did they, Dad?"

"No. I don't think we made it that far."

"They seemed to think we didn't belong here," Gulliver said.

"Imagine that." Toby shook his head, shooing them into the library, where Xavier and several of the local fae leaders were crowded around one of the human screen gadgets they were always staring at.

"Look, Dad." Gulliver pointed at the screen. "We're on the human feletision."

"How?" Griffin looked behind him the way they'd come. "We were just out there talking to that nice lady, and now we're on the human screen?" He leaned toward the small tablet. "Can you hear us?"

"What. Did. You. Just. Do?" Xavier growled, and Toby laid a hand on his arm, shaking his head and muttering something like, "don't bother."

"Who are the idiots?" a really scary-looking woman asked.

Toby sighed. "I've never seen these two before in my life."

Chapter Eighteen
SOPHIE-ANN

You must decide which side you're on.

Sophie stared up at the white ceiling, looking for patterns in the old stains from long ago leaks. Yesterday, she found one that held a remarkable resemblance to the Statue of Liberty, but she couldn't find it again this morning.

The game reminded her of better times. Before her mother died, and they'd visited one of the many parks near their home in the Quarter. Sophie and her mother used to lay on a blanket, looking up at the clouds for familiar shapes.

Once again, she found herself dreaming of a life where her mother never died in a blast of magic. A life where Sophie-Ann Devereaux grew up with a mother and a father who adored her, living in a world that never grew dark and had never known the touch of fae magic.

Sighing, she rolled onto her side, facing the door that had yet to open in the two days since her father had dragged her in here. Her stomach gnawed at her insides, and she tried not to think about food. They'd given her water, at least, but no amount of it filled the aching hunger inside her.

She'd lost all sense of time without a window to see the sun rise and set. Claude Devereaux wanted her to pick a side, but Sophie had a hard time aligning herself with someone who would do such a thing to his own daughter.

Staring at the shimmer of light under the door, Sophie busied herself with watching for passing feet. Only a few pairs had gone by her cell throughout the day, and none of them had stopped.

Her eyelids started to droop again, and she groaned irritably. She'd had enough sleep to last her a lifetime. The world was falling to pieces, and she needed to get out there to do her part. She sat up and rubbed her eyes, searching the tiny room for a way out. But over the last two days, she'd studied every crevice in the room, and she was stuck.

Shadows moved by the door and paused.

Sophie held her breath, hoping someone would finally open that door and tell her that her father had made a mistake. That he loved her too much to lock her up like this.

A key slid into the lock, and the knob turned slowly, as if her visitor was trying very hard not to make a noise.

"Dad?" She stood hesitantly as her father stepped into the room, a grim look of determination on his face.

"We have to get you to the doctor, Sophie-Ann." He reached for her arm, not meeting her gaze as he unceremoniously marched her from the room.

"Dad, wait." She tried to move from his grasp, but his fingers wrapped tightly around her arm, refusing to let go. "Why are you doing this?"

"It's not safe. We have to get you help." He ushered her down the empty corridor to an exit, where Gabe waited with a car.

"I'm perfectly fine," she tried to explain. "I've been hea—"

"Don't say it!" he hissed, shoving her into the back seat of a silver sedan. "Do not say those filthy words again." He slammed the door in her face and snatched the keys from Gabe.

For the first time ever, Sophie wished Gabe would come with them. She stared at the man she was supposed to marry and found sympathy there.

Gabe laid a palm on the window and mouthed the words, 'I'm sorry', before her father pulled away.

They drove in silence for a while, Sophie in the backseat and her estranged father in the front. He drove too fast, muttering to himself until she worked up the courage to speak.

"Where are we going, Dad?"

"Just be quiet, Sophie-Ann." He sounded so weary and defeated. "We are going to fix this."

"There is nothing to be fixed. Not with me."

But he refused to say any more.

They arrived at a small clinic on the outskirts of Los Angeles. Her father screeched to a halt in a parking spot by the door and was out of the front seat almost before he had the car in park.

He opened the door and reached in to lift Sophie out. Just like all the other times he'd taken her to the hospital or the many clinics they'd visited when she was at her sickest.

"I can walk on my own." She tried to twist out of his arms, but he held her tight.

"It's Saturday, but Dr. Anderson has agreed to see you. We won't have to wait long, and then we'll be back at headquarters, where you can rest."

"I don't need rest. I'm fine." She was about to get really

angry if her father put her through rounds of unnecessary tests and treatments she didn't need.

"Please." He hugged her close as they stepped into the dark waiting room of the clinic. "Just be patient. We have to do this."

"Ah, there's our girl." Dr. Anderson gestured for them to follow him down a long narrow hall. "How's she feeling?"

"She's not herself," her father answered for her.

"She's fine," Sophie added. "This isn't necessary."

"Let's just start with a few scans, shall we?" Dr. Anderson stepped into a sterile room, and her father laid her on the MRI machine.

"Just relax, Sophie-Ann." The doctor flashed a light in her eyes and checked her pulse. "Nice and steady. Good." He put a stethoscope in his ears and laid the circular chest piece against her skin. "Good, good. Heart sounds perfect."

"I really don't need—"

"Sophie-Ann, just cooperate. We have to do this." Her father paced the cold white room.

"Mr. Devereaux, you'll need to wait outside while we run the scans." A technician waited behind a wall of windows to start the machine.

"You know the drill, sweetheart. Lie still, and it'll be over soon." Her dad left the room, closing the door behind him.

"Really, Doctor, this isn't necessary."

"You have Leukemia. We need to see what's going on before we can continue your treatment."

"Fine." She laid back, giving herself a minute to relax. She really hated MRIs. It felt like getting buried alive.

For the rest of the afternoon, they poked her, X-rayed her, and drew blood to run every kind of test known to man. Her father was determined to believe she was still dying of Leukemia.

Finally, the doctor came back into her room, where her father had insisted she lay on the bed like a sick patient.

"Good news and bad news." Dr. Anderson moved to sit on a round stool by her bed. "The good news is, she isn't sick. At all. There are no signs of Leukemia."

"So, she's in remission?" Her father's voice filled with hope. "The last treatments worked?"

"No. And that's the bad news, Claude." The doctor turned to her father. "There is no sign that Sophie was ever sick. No signs of Leukemia or any other illness. Her scans show a girl who has never been sick a day in her life. She has no scars, no signs of the broken wrist she had when she was seven. There isn't a scratch on her. She's in perfect health."

"Blasted fae!" Her dad punched a fist right through the drywall.

"Dad!" Sophie scrambled out of the bed.

"I'm sorry to have to give you such news, Claude. I know it's not what you wanted to hear." Dr. Anderson laid a reassuring hand on her father's shoulder before he left the room.

"Why does it sound like you'd rather me be on death's door?" Sophie reached for her stack of clothes, ready to get out of this place.

Claude stood with his back to her, staring with unseeing eyes out the window. "I'd rather you be dead than one of them."

Sophie tugged her jeans on under her hospital gown. "I'm not one of them. They can't just make someone fae."

"You're full of their magic."

"I've been healed with their magic, but that's a good thing, Dad. It means I get to live my life. They are not the evil creatures you think they are."

A tear slid down her father's face, and he reached to wipe

it away, shaking his head. "They tainted you with their magic. You belong to them now."

"I don't belong to anyone." Anger welled within her. "I'm an adult, and the only one I have to answer to is myself."

"Just get dressed. I'll take you home." Her father's shoulders slumped as he left the room.

The drive back to the HAFS headquarters was a silent one. No amount of pestering him would get her father to speak to her.

"You're not putting me back in that room. I won't go." Sophie watched the palm trees streak past her window as they neared the building. If she had to, she would run. She was a lot stronger than her father realized.

But they drove right past the giant square building.

"Where are you taking me?" She watched as the building faded behind them, and her father turned down a side street.

"I can't do it." Her father's shoulders shuddered. "I can't."

"Can't do what, Dad?" Sophie leaned over the front seat. "You have to tell me what's happening."

"It'll be okay, Sophie-Ann, sweetheart. I-I'll fix this. There has to be a way."

He turned down a tree-lined drive and pulled through automatic iron gates that swung open and closed behind them. He glanced back at her, as if he expected some reaction from her. "Are you all right?" The iron doesn't … hurt you, does it?"

"Wait, what … Dad, I haven't been turned into a fae." She rolled her eyes when she realized what he was asking. "They aren't vampires. I'm me. Same Sophie I've always been but healthy." She decided not to tell him that iron didn't affect the fae as he believed.

"No." He shook his head, his eyes bulging with fear. "No, that's not true." He stopped the car in front of a stucco Spanish-style mansion with a red-tiled roof. It was beautiful, but there was no way her father could afford to stay in such a place.

"Who lives here? Where have you brought me?" She refused to get out of the car when he opened the back door. With the tall iron gates around the property, running was out of the question.

"Sophie?" Gabe came jogging out the front door and down the steps. "Is she all right?" He pushed past her father and peered into the backseat. "How are you feeling, Soph?"

"I'm fine." She moved deeper into the backseat, fully aware they could force her out the other side, but she had nowhere to hide.

"You're really, okay?" His voice squeaked with relief. "You're not dying?"

"No."

"Get her into the house." Her father barked a command and left them in the driveway as he made his way up the stairs like he owned the place.

"Who lives here?" she demanded again.

"It's a HAFS rental," Gabe explained, trying to coax her out of the backseat. "A bunch of the HAFS leaders are staying here while we deal with these fae who think they can just claim L.A. for themselves. I can't believe it. It's all over the news." He leaned into the car. "You have to come inside with me. You have a room here. A real one. I'll try to catch you up if they let me." His eyes filled with worry. "I really am so happy you're back and that you're well. It's a miracle." He reached to grasp her hand. "Even if it is a fae miracle." He squeezed her hand gently. "I'll make sure you're safe here, Soph. Your dad is just really worried about you."

He couldn't seem to stop staring at her as he helped her from the car. It was the gentlest he'd ever been with her, even compared to when she was dying in the hospital. She had no choice but to go with him.

Her eyes didn't know what to look at as they entered the beautiful home, with its curved staircase leading up from the Spanish foyer to an open upstairs landing.

Her room was beautiful. With a comfortable-looking bed and a window overlooking well-manicured gardens.

It also came with locked doors and bars obstructing the view.

Chapter Nineteen
TOBY

Toby paced the length of the Aghadoon library, trying not to remember all the times he'd seen his father and uncle do the same thing as they searched for a way to destroy Egan and save the human realm from the darkness he'd unleashed on them.

"They say a man turns into his father," he muttered. He was alone, thankfully, and able to think of his family back in Iskalt. What would Tia do if Griffin put her in the spot he'd just put all the fae in? His father, he knew, would go running to Griffin and bash his head against the pavement until his brother told him he knew what an idiot he'd been.

But violence was something Tia inherited more than Toby. He'd always been more of a talk-it-out kind of fae, which was ironic considering he found himself among the leaders of one side in a brewing war.

The time for talk was through.

Orla barged through the door, stopping when she saw Toby. "Are you going to do something about this?" She was the leader of the Los Angeles fae, but she knew so little of the actual fae world that it would have been funny in different circumstances.

"I'm not sure what you think I can accomplish here." Toby collapsed into a high-backed, ornate wooden chair. The library had never been comfortable, looking too ancient to exist in these times.

"He's your uncle. Deal with him." The fae leader thumped a fist on the table. She looked out of place in her jeans and t-shirt, and Toby had a sudden feeling that the library was too good for the likes of her. He'd tried not to regret asking his grandfather for help in a human war, but he couldn't help feeling like none of the fae in this world belonged in a place such as this.

And Toby was through with the disrespect. He stood once again, rising to his full height, his jaw tightening.

"I am a prince of the fae realm. You currently stand in our most sacred source of knowledge, so you will treat me as such. As for my uncle, he too carries royal fae blood. He made a mistake, but it was one born of ignorance, not ill will. We will overcome the stumble, and we will do it with his help." He moved around the table until he was face to face with Orla. "Griffin O'Shea helped save your little human world from the darkness you all fear so much, and you don't even realize it. He has been through more than you could fathom, and still, he is here to help. If you don't appreciate his aid, I will send him away. Because I will not let him be disrespected by the likes of you." He bumped the woman's shoulder on the way out of the library.

A slow drizzle wet the village, casting the mood into a gloomy stupor. All they could do was wait. As news crews hounded anyone who set foot outside the village walls and the human shows ran cycle after cycle of anti-fae rhetoric, they sat here waiting for their moment.

Not knowing what that moment was.

Toby walked through the center of town, keeping his eyes on his feet to avoid meeting the distrusting gazes surrounding him. This wasn't like Iskalt, where the fae may have walked cautiously around him but still respected him. Here, they'd started treating him like the humans treated them. Ever since Griffin's mistaken words, they whispered about the full-blooded fae in their midst who didn't belong.

Maybe they were right.

Toby entered the small cottage his grandfather called home, needing to speak with the one man who wouldn't tell him he was imagining the change in the air. Brandon O'Rourke sat at a small four-person wooden table in the kitchen. Here, everything looked as it would in the fae realm, and it gave Toby a strange sort of comfort. Being in Aghadoon made him miss Iskalt in a way he hadn't been sure he would.

"Grandfather?" He hesitated in the doorway.

Brandon looked up, his reading glasses askew. He had a worn book in front of him with yellowed pages and a leather cover. "Ah, Toby. Come in, my boy." His genuine smile was like a balm to a burn Toby hadn't realized he had.

He moved into the room and took an open seat.

Brandon stood. "I'll make us some tea. You look like you could use it."

Tea. Thank the magic. In the human realm, everyone was so obsessed with coffee. It tasted too much like the Eldur brew his mother once tried to get him to fall in love with. Toby even hated the smell.

Brandon set a steaming cup of tea that held a familiar scent. Toby looked up at him. "Fargelsian tea?" Made in Fargelsi with an abundance of Gelsi berries, no fae with magic drank it for fear it would dampen their power. Only the magic-less like Toby, who normally joined the servant class, or those in Myrkur and Lenya, whose power worked differently, got to enjoy the delicious aromas.

Brandon smiled. "I don't have much use for my magic in Aghadoon, so I don't deprive myself of the best tea on the market."

Toby inhaled deeply before taking a sip and sighing. "It tastes like home."

Brandon set his mug on the table and studied Toby in that scrutinizing way of his. "Have you talked to your sister?"

He lifted one shoulder in a shrug. "Griff no longer has the journals. I don't have a way to communicate with her."

The knowing look from his grandfather was enough for Toby to guess what the man thought about that. Toby had the strongest portal magic—his only magic—in the O'Shea family. If he wanted to see Tia, he could. With a sigh, he set his tea down. "She won't want to see me."

"And why is that?"

"Because I didn't return with Gullie. I was kind of awful to him."

"Has Gullie forgiven you?"

"Well, we haven't talked about it, but he doesn't seem mad. That's Gullie, though. He'd never hold a grudge. I just ..." He couldn't voice the words. He didn't want to see Tia's disappointment in him. And she'd be right. Because of him, the fae world was dragged into this conflict. He shouldn't be there ready to fight, neither should Gullie nor Griff. And Aghadoon ... it belonged nowhere near the human realm. But right now, it was an anchor they needed. A way to show their might without a blatant attack on the humans, but at the same time it offered a refuge for the innocent fae who needed protection.

"Ah." Brandon nodded. "I see. You're afraid she'll forgive you too."

"Why would I …" His voice trailed off. Was that the truth? He and Tia had once been so close it was like they were one soul in two bodies. Even their power was connected. He might not have magic other than the ability to open portals, but when her power flowed through him, he amplified it.

And then, there was last year. He could feel her from a great distance. He knew when she was okay and when she was coming home.

None of that mattered anymore when Logan died and Toby shut himself off from everyone, including his twin sister. He didn't realize it until right then, but the hole inside him wasn't only there because he'd lost the man he loved.

He'd lost his sister too.

That, at least, was his fault.

"Grandfather, how do you do that?"

"Do what?" A smirk appeared on his lips, but he tried to hide it with his mug. The man looked no older than forty, but his eyes betrayed his age with a wisdom in them few had.

"You always know what I'm feeling before I do."

"It's because I love you, kid. From the day you were born and I held your slimy body in my arms."

"Gross."

"It's life. Get over it." His smile grew. "I've always been a man with a purpose. I was raised to be the king, then I was a prisoner, and finally, the man inside Aghadoon, who had to have all the answers. I didn't choose any of it. But with the arrival of you and your siblings … along with your cousins in Fargelsi … being a grandfather is a greater calling than anything else. I have spent hours upon hours just watching you as a child, learning your facial expressions, your fears, and your loves. That's also how I know your sister has already forgiven you. I know her too. You need not be afraid of that forgiveness."

"What if I don't deserve it?"

"That's the thing about love, Toby. Sometimes, forgiveness comes first. It's on us to deserve it later."

Two heavy thumps on the door ended their conversation. Brandon stood to see who it was and returned a moment later with a harried-looking Orla. She was out of breath, as if she'd run all the way here.

"Toby, have you seen Xavier?" she asked, wheezing.

"No." Toby stood, sensing something wasn't right. "What happened?"

"May... she's dead."

One of Xavier's earliest allies against HAFS. "Does he know?" Alarm ravaged him, worry for the woman he'd come to care about.

Orla nodded. "He took off, and now I can't find him."

"I know where he is." Without another word, Toby raced from the house and weaved through the streets of Aghadoon. Near the back wall of the village, there was a small alcove, protected from the rain by the overhang from a nearby shop. Xavier showed it to him a few days ago. It was the one place he could go where no one could find him.

Sometimes, this crowded village became too much for Xavier, and he needed some space. But not from Toby. He'd brought him here, and that had to mean something, right?

He was almost there when he saw him. Xavier sat on the dusty cobblestone, his back leaning against the shop next door. He had his legs bent, his arms resting on his knees, and his head hanging between them. Sitting impossibly still, he didn't sob or shake.

Toby slipped under the overhang and shook water out of

his hair. He looked down at his friend, at the bowed crown of his head. Leaning against the wall opposite Xavier, Toby slid down until he sat across from him, their knees bumping together in the small space.

"They're all gone," Xavier whispered, lifting his stricken face. There were no tears, but the grief was there. "Everyone I care about. My mother. My grandparents. May They've all died because of this hatred."

Toby wasn't sure what to say for a moment, so he scooted forward, pushing Xavier's knees apart so he could crouch in front of him. "Not everyone." He reached forward, tilting Xavier's chin until their eyes met. "I'm still here."

Xavier shook him off, scooting away. "But for how long? Huh, Toby? When will you leave me too? This isn't your world. Eventually, you'll go home."

Tears gathered in Toby's eyes. "Do you really not see it?" He hadn't been this close to anyone since Logan. It felt like a betrayal, but he couldn't help wanting Xavier, wanting the closeness he'd once experienced. Logan wasn't here anymore, but Toby still had a life to live.

"The day the boy I loved died," he started. "I thought I wanted to die right along with him. Until recently, I still did." He'd never talked about this with anyone. "I understand exactly how you feel, Xavier. Your friend is gone, and I'm more sorry than you know for that. Nothing we can do will bring her back. That is the cost of war, and I've experienced it too often. But we're still here. We still have to fight. We still have to live."

"I don't know if I have any more fight in me."

"You do." Toby had never seen anyone become a leader as quickly as Xavier, and that included Tia. She'd taken quite a bit of time. But him ... it was like he was meant to guide these fae to safety, bring them to peace. Toby refused to let him give up. "Do you know how I know that?"

Xavier shook his head.

"Because I have fight in me." He reached for Xavier's hand, wrapping his around it, sliding their fingers together. "Earlier tonight, I wondered if I belonged here, but it only took a single moment for me to realize I do."

"How?" Xavier shook his head. "How do you know this is your fight?"

Toby got the impression his answer mattered more than it seemed, that the words he used right now could help Xavier off this cliff or make him jump. "Because it's yours."

Xavier's eyes snapped to his, a single tear trailing down his cheek. "She's really gone, Tobes."

"I know. But you aren't alone." He pulled Xavier into his arms, tightening his embrace until Xavier relaxed into the hug. "I will never leave you, not unless you want me to." Toby didn't know where the words came from or why they didn't hurt like he expected them to. "We're in this together."

Xavier rested his chin on Toby's shoulder. "Thank you."

Xavier shouldn't have been the one thanking him, but Toby didn't say that. Instead, he looked to the sky, wondering if Logan watched over him. *I'm sorry, Logan.* He let the thought drift away into the past. *I love you, but there is more in this life for me, and I have to live it.*

Maybe his grandfather was right. That forgiveness he was sure Tia had already given him ... he could still earn it.

Chapter Twenty
SOPHIE-ANN

"Who knows what's next?"

Sophie watched the replay of Griff's interview on the news, still not able to believe he'd actually said those words. If she'd never met a fae, never seen their palaces, their thriving world, she might have taken them the same way the people around her did.

She might have thought the fae wanted to rule over the human world.

"He's such an idiot," she muttered, rubbing her eyes.

"What?" Gabe asked from his place on the couch beside her. He was today's assigned guard, the unlucky soul who had to keep the human infected with fae magic from ... Well, from what, Sophie wasn't exactly sure. What did they think she'd do?

She was lucky it was Gabe today. As much as she disliked him still, he was the only guard who let her out of her room to watch the news and catch up on everything she'd missed. "Nothing."

"You know that animal?" Gabe pointed at Griff's image on the screen.

Sophie rolled her eyes. "I was in their world for a grand total of like five seconds. I didn't meet every single fae. So, no, Gabe. I don't know him," she lied.

He seemed to relax at that. "Well, Claude and the rest are at headquarters right now, deciding how to handle things with such a blatant threat. We've been too easy on them so far."

Easy on them? Was that what he called the bombings, the massed HAFS army outside L.A.? Because that's what they'd become in her absence. HAFS wasn't just a fringe conspiracy group anymore. They'd turned into a fighting force, with the full backing of many governments and the majority of the people. It was frightening.

"What do you think they'll do?" she asked, keeping her voice soft the way he liked it. Gabe may have been the only one happy to see her when she returned, but that didn't mean he'd changed. He still wanted to force her into marriage, still wanted her to be the meek girl he'd known.

Sophie had news for him. That girl was gone.

He shrugged. "Fight, I guess. We were planning an attack, but they'll probably move up the timeline. We have to get to them before they're ready for us. HAFS may have the numbers, but the one thing we don't have is magic."

The truth sat there in front of her, a truth that would change everything for HAFS and let them know they'd win this fight.

Most of the half-fae had little magic to speak of. The ones who did only displayed weak power. Griffin was most likely the only real danger to HAFS and only at night.

Something kept her from revealing these secrets. In all their worry over whether she was turning into a fae because of the healing magic—a ridiculous notion—not a single person had thought to ask if she'd learned anything useful. They underestimated her once again, and they'd pay for it.

"What on earth is that?" She leaned forward as the news showed a flash of light and then the appearance of a medieval-looking town right inside L.A. It was old footage, not live, but it kept her entranced.

Gabe scooted closer, his arm stretched over the back of the couch. Sophie knew what he was doing, but she could only focus on the news replay.

"We're not completely sure." Gabe's fingertips grazed her shoulder, and she suppressed a cringe. "It just appeared one day, and we can't get any of our people inside."

Magic. It had to be. The news feed switched to an aerial view of the village, with an icon in the corner that told watchers it was live footage.

"I don't understand." She'd meant the words for herself, but Gabe didn't seem to realize it.

"None of us do, but what do we really know about the fae in this other world? Only that they want to destroy us, right? They're animals."

He couldn't be more wrong. She thought of Tia and her parents. Of Griffin. Gulliver. The fae were as sophisticated as any human. They used their magic the way humans used technology, and only when they had to. Their lives were not altogether different from humans. They had families, fell in love, and just wanted to survive from one day to the next.

But this ... magical village ... it was beyond anything she'd imagined. Crumbling pillars marked an entryway that looked surrounded by men and women carrying heavy weapons. The L.A. fae were said to be more militarized than others, more organized. It made sense. They had so much to protect.

Fae scampered about the village, talking in groups. The

camera zoomed in on one building in particular, where fae came and went continuously. Sophie wasn't sure how long she sat there watching the feed or what she was waiting for. Not until she saw him.

A sob lodged in her throat. Gulliver. He was there. He looked to the sky, as if staring right into the camera, right into her eyes. There must have been a helicopter or drone circling the village, gathering footage, but everything stopped.

He looked like he had the day she met him in the cafe. No tail, human-looking eyes. Kind face.

Yet ... that wasn't him. In her mind, she saw a different man. One who risked everything to save her, was best friends with everyone he saw, and spoke to her through a wall just to tell her everything she'd needed to hear.

She only wished she'd had more words for him.

The man in her head wasn't human, and looking like one stole the character from him. She missed the tail that seemed to have a mind of its own, the narrow cat-like eyes that saw every part of her.

Gabe was watching Sophie, studying her, and she drew back into the couch, regretting it instantly. His arm dropped down, coming around her. She hated it with the passion of a thousand separate worlds, but she did her best not to shy away. He was the key.

If he still had feelings for her, still wanted her, he might help when the time was right.

Yet, there it was again, scrolling across the bottom of the screen as they continued to show the village. *"Who knows what's next?"*

"Gabe?" she asked, looking up at him with an innocent expression.

"Yeah?" He played with a lock of her hair.

"Do you think they meant it? That the fae truly want our world?"

He paused for a moment, his hand going still. "I don't know."

"But—"

"Xavier used to tell me rumors about the fae world."

There was a time Gabe and his half-brother didn't hate each other, a time they'd been family when neither had much of that.

Gabe continued. "He said his father knew someone who'd lived there. A woman named Enis. He spoke of kingdoms full of castles and magic, a place where war had ended."

"Do you believe him?"

"I don't know." His voice quieted, as if he was afraid of anyone else hearing. "But what I do wonder ... if the fae have such an amazing world, what would they want with ours?"

It was in the way he said it, the doubt in his voice. Sophie had never expected to find a semi-ally in Gabe, but, like her, he knew the fae weren't a threat to them.

At least now.

That was the problem, wasn't it? While Tia ruled in Iskalt and kept the other monarchs informed, she wouldn't march here and claim what she could take with a flick of her magic. But she wouldn't rule forever, and the humans couldn't protect themselves against the kind of power full-blooded fae wielded.

Magic wasn't distinctly evil, but it had no place in a world of humans. It never would.

War wasn't the solution, but then, what was?

"I'm a little tired." She pushed herself up from the couch. "I think I'll go lie down."

She didn't give him a chance to protest before sprinting up the stairs to the room she'd been given.

There was a loose board in the floor she'd found the day before, and she pried it up to pull out the journal that connected her to the one person who'd know how to end this.

Opening the book, she stared at the blank page. Tia told her anything she wrote would make it to the identical book in Tia's possession. She'd said a fae would then normally erase what they'd written with their magic, but Sophie would have to just leave it and flip to a new blank page each time.

She pulled open the drawer of the dusty desk and dug through it until she found a pen, one that didn't look like it had been used in quite some time. Testing it on the page, she started writing.

Tia,

You might want to talk to Griff.

Tia's response came almost immediately.

What did he do now?

She barely knew the queen, but she could almost imagine the affectionate sigh in her voice. There was a lot of love for her family. *Just tell him he might not want to speak to reporters and say he wants to take over the human world.*

She could picture Tia's pacing, hear the curses rolling off her tongue. Sophie couldn't help it. She liked the queen. In a different life, they could have been friends.

Finally, Tia responded.

I'll handle him. Do you have any other news for me?

Sophie didn't want to betray her father or the other humans. She only wanted peace. *I think they're going to move up any attacks. We ...* She paused, not sure how much she should say. *Human sentiment has turned against the fae. HAFS even has the government's full attention now.*

Sophie waited for Tia's response to that, but it didn't

come. She wondered if she angered the queen somehow, but she couldn't worry about that right now, not when there was so much at stake.

She needed to find a way to make both sides realize they weren't so different, make them realize peace was easier than war.

Magic didn't belong here, but what about the fae without magic? They weren't even recognizable as something other than human. She'd always imagined this world to have a place for anyone to live the kind of life they wanted. Even when corrupted by hate and bloodshed, there were corners of the planet where peace reigned.

Was that even possible anymore? Or would HAFS not rest until every single one of the fae was gone from their world?

Chapter Twenty-One
GULLIVER

"What do you mean, we're grounded?" Gulliver blinked up at Xavier from his seat at the table in the Aghadoon library.

"We took a vote," Orla said. "It was unanimous. You two aren't allowed to leave Aghadoon. We can't risk you two *accidentally* talking to a reporter again."

"We can't leave at all? Not even for tacos?" Gulliver gaped at the group of stern faces.

"I think we messed up," Griffin whisper shouted. "But I'm sure we can get someone to bring us tacos."

"Can't we send them back to their queen?" Orla growled.

"Hey, my queen sent me here to help you." Gulliver's tail twitched behind him. Others might not be able to see his Dark Fae features, but they were still there. "If it weren't for me, you wouldn't have our help right now."

"We were doing just fine without you," Orla shot back.

"That's enough." Xavier banged his fist on the table. "We need both Gulliver and Griffin for important reasons. Griffin is one of our only magic wielders, and he's an O'Shea who can open portals."

"And Gulliver is our connection to Sophie," Toby added. "And through her, Claude Devereaux and his followers."

"That might be helpful if I knew where she was." Gulliver's tail wilted to the floor at the mention of Sophie's name. He missed her. But Tia had sent her back home like she wanted. And Gullie wasn't sure he'd ever even see her again. Maybe he was just in the way here.

As the meeting broke up and everyone went about their important tasks, Gulliver sank lower into his chair. The chair beside him moved and someone sat down. "I have a project for you, Gul," Toby said in hushed tones. "You too, Uncle Griff."

"One that doesn't involve leaving or either of us doing anything remotely useful?" Gulliver muttered.

"Actually, it could prove to be a vital tool to our mission." Toby set a human screen device in front of him.

Gulliver shoved away from the table. "No way am I touching that."

"It's not a good idea, Tobes. I've broken a few of those things, and your mother won't let me use hers anymore," Griffin said.

"It's not as difficult as it seems. Er, maybe you can just help Gullie with ideas. Mom taught me a few things on her phone, and this tablet is just like a big phone. Humans use it to research things—and play games."

"Games?" Gulliver inched forward.

"That's not important right now. We need to find Sophie, and we have no idea where she's gone since Tia sent her back home. All we know is she's not at her house in New Orleans."

"And no one else has the time to track her down," Griffin added.

"How do we use this tablet thing to find her?" Gilliver tapped on the screen like he'd seen others do, but it didn't light up for him.

"I forget what makes it do that." Toby picked up the electronic paper and shook it.

"Don't do that." Xavier came back to the table with a stack of books and snatched the tablet from Toby. "It's an iPad. When it's dark like that, it means the power isn't on. Just push the button on the bottom."

"Oh, right." Toby took it back and tapped the button, and the screen lit up with a funny looking apple.

"I'm not so sure you should be the one teaching them to do this." Xavier nudged Toby aside and perched on the edge of his chair between Toby and Gulliver.

Gulliver listened intently as Xavier went over how to turn the iPad on, how to charge it when it lost power, and how to search for things with a button called Google. He showed them all the news apps and how to search for the latest information. And he taught them about social media. Something called Faceplace and clocktok. Xavier told them how to use hashtags and forbid them from using the camera to record anything. He even put something called a sticker over the camera so no one could see them. Gullie just wasn't sure how the human contraption could see anything.

"Just see what you can find that could be important to us. Obscure things the mainstream media isn't reporting on." Xavier quickly scribbled down a list of hashtags for them to search, and then he and Toby left them to it.

"Want to search for a taco delivery place?" Griffin moved to sit beside his son. "We're going to need sustenance."

"Let's look for news on Sophie, and then we can ask the Google guy to bring us food." Gulliver tapped on the Google button and typed in #WhereIsSophieDevereaux.

"Wow, all that is about Sophie?" Griffin leaned in to study the list of news articles and videos about Sophie's mysterious disappearance from the hospital.

"*Fae are involved*," read one article on a place called Feed the Buzz. "*The girl was minutes from death, according to her doctors. Then, poof! She disappears only to return the picture of health? Either Sophie Devereaux is fae herself, or she has very powerful fae friends*.

"Hey, that's you!" Griffin nudged Gulliver. "You're her powerful fae friend."

All the articles said the same thing. After returning out of the blue, in perfect health, Sophie vanished from the public eye. Her last sighting was here in Los Angeles.

"She went right back to her father," Gulliver murmured.

"That doesn't make her our enemy, son." Griffin laid a hand on his shoulder. "It just means, no matter what awful things Claude Devereaux has done in his past, his daughter still loves him."

"Yeah, but the difference between you and Claude is you turned your life around long before you found me. You did bad things in your past, but you grew up and you found your way. Claude is an evil man. Through and through."

"And if I were still an evil man, you would still love me because I'm your father," Griffin said softly. "Give her a chance to do the right thing."

Gulliver nodded and tapped on a video from the clocktik place. A young woman who called herself TheNOLASpirit came on screen, and for a second Gulliver thought she was dark fae with her bunny ears and nose with whiskers, but he suspected it was some sort of human joke he didn't get. In this realm, even if she was like him, he wouldn't have been able to see it.

"Hashtag where is Sophie Deveraux?" the girl said. "I'll

tell you where she is. That father of hers has her locked up somewhere. Back when HAFS first formed in the weeks after the darkness came to New Orleans, my parents were founding members. I was in high school at the time, so I didn't get to go to the real meetings, but I knew Sophie back then. I even babysat her frequently during HAFS meetings. She was a sweet girl. Very timid and shy. When my parents realized Claude Devereaux was off his rocker, they quit the group. We never saw them again, but that man keeps a tight rein on his daughter. More people need to be asking #WhereIsSophieDevereaux because wherever she is, it isn't good. If Sophie was healed by the fae, Claude will punish her for her involvement. And lots of people go missing around that man."

Gulliver shared a look with his father. "None of the news places are reporting anything like that about Sophie."

"They've forgotten her." Gulliver tapped on another video on the FacePlace and heard more of the same. A lot of people were worried about Sophie and what her father might do to her. "Grounded or not, we have to find her, Dad."

"We will." Griffin pried the iPad out of Gulliver's hands. "But first we need tacos."

Gullie didn't have much of an appetite. After only three tacos, he turned down the fourth. "I need to talk to Toby."

The door to the library crashed open, and both Gullie and Griff flinched.

"Don't do that, Xavier," Gullie gasped. "I thought the humans were throwing their bombs at us."

"You spent forty-eight dollars on tacos?" Xavier fumed.

"What, is that bad?" Gulliver winced. "We weren't sure how to stick the money card into your tablet thing."

"You realize I'm not wealthy, right? I'm not a fae prince with loads of gold or whatever you people value."

"Xavier." Toby came in behind him, gasping for breath. "What did they do this time?"

"They charged their dinner to my account."

"We did?" Griffin's eyes widened. "I told you it wasn't free!" He turned on Gulliver.

"It never asked for money. It's not my fault." He shoved the iPad at his father.

"To be fair, it was your idea to give them your tablet." Toby didn't hide his smile.

"I didn't know they were going to clean me out."

"Here, my good lad, this should cover it." Griffin stood up and fished a few fire opals from his pocket. "That should more than cover what we spent. It was an accident, truly."

"You two have lots of food-related accidents," Xavier muttered, studying the opals. "What are these anyway? It's not like I can deposit them at my bank in *New Orleans*, seeing as how we're in Los Angeles."

"Deposit?" Griffin frowned. "I don't think there are any impure deposits in the opals. They are quite valuable, I assure you. Particularly in Lenya."

"I will make it up to you," Toby interrupted before Xavier could really explode. "I'll ask my mother to make a contribution to your accounts. She knows all about human money."

"Fine, but I'm taking my iPad. I don't need them discovering my amazon account." Xavier snatched the device and stomped from the library.

Griffin stood, studying the fading afternoon sunset. "I better go see Brea soon. She'll make it right for us.

"Make it a quick trip, Griff. We really do need you here,"

Toby said.

"I'll hop back after the Iskaltian sun sets." Griffin stepped outside to open his portal in the village square.

"Things would be a lot easier if more people could portal." Gulliver sighed. "I don't suppose you'd send me to Sophie?"

"I would if I knew where she was." Toby sank down onto the chair beside Gullie.

"There's no real news of her on any of these pages. But there is a lot of speculation about her location. Some believe she's with her father—that he's done something to her as punishment for her involvement with the fae. I'm afraid Tia might have sent her into the lion's den, and Sophie is so clouded by her love for her father she can't see that's the worst place she could be. I need to go find her, Tobes."

Toby heaved a sigh and ran a hand through his hair. "It was her choice to go back to him."

"I know, but I need to make sure she's okay."

"I think you would know if she wasn't," Toby said, refusing to meet his eyes.

"What do you mean?"

"Griffin doesn't have Tia's journal. The one he was supposed to give me the last time I saw him. I asked him for it so I could send my sister a message."

"So what? He left it in Iskalt?"

"Someone else has it," Toby said. "I made Griffin tell me."

"Who has it, Tobes?" Gulliver gripped the edge of the table.

"Sophie. Tia gave it to her so she could keep us informed. If she needs help, we will know."

"And no one thought I might be the best fae to keep in contact with her? That she might trust me more than a queen she's terrified of?" Gulliver flew out of his chair, his tail sweeping the books from the table to the floor. Tia had a direct line to Sophie and she'd just let him worry?

"Tia probably thought it would be too much of a distraction for you. I agree. You need to forget about this human girl, and let Tia handle the communication."

"Oh, so you two are teaming up against me now?" Gulliver wanted to scream he was so angry.

"Your judgment isn't always the best where Sophie's concerned."

"Seriously, Toby, I could punch you right now ... but I'm scared of our crazy sister." Gulliver slumped back down in his seat, defeated.

Toby snorted a laugh. "You and me both, Gul. Tia's frustrated she can't be here in the thick of it. The spelled journals give her a way to be involved. Part of her wants us here to be her eyes and ears, but she doesn't actually want us doing anything that will get us hurt."

"But it's Sophie." Gulliver sighed. "I can't just leave her in the enemy's hands. I can't sit around and wait for Tia to get a message from Sophie when she's in Iskalt and unable to react quickly enough. Even if her father does love her, I don't trust that Gabe guy."

"How do you know we can trust her?"

"There is something good in Sophie. She's not like her father. And I need you to trust my judgment and my intuition. She's the key to everything, and I need to find her. Sooner than later."

"I trust you, Gul." Toby finally nodded. "I'll help you, but I'm just not sure I can see the good in anyone anymore."

"Not even Xavier?" Gullie teased, and Toby blushed bright red before he punched Gulliver's shoulder so hard he flipped out of his chair.

Chapter Twenty-Two
SOPHIE-ANN

Sophie was going stir crazy inside the HAFS headquarters house in Los Angeles. People came and went at all hours of the day and night, but no one paid Sophie any mind. She was just the ditzy daughter of the New Orleans leader, who'd gotten herself wrapped up with the enemy and couldn't be trusted.

Most ignored her.

Some made their hate for her painfully clear. And others wholeheartedly believed she was tainted with fae magic.

Her only source of outside information was the news that played on the main television, and Gabe. He was the only guard who would talk to her. When Gabe wasn't there, Sophie was locked in her room with nothing to do but stare at the stains on the ceiling.

But today he was here, and Sophie got to sit beside the pool with him, presumably enjoying the California sunshine, hiding behind her sunglasses and a tabloid magazine. Gabe dozed in the lounge beside her, leaving her free to study those coming and going across the lawn from the garage to the house and back.

Stern faces wore grim expressions as men and women came to receive their marching orders from the leaders of HAFS. Sophie took note when guns were involved. And there were *a lot* of guns. The garage had been converted into an armory, and trucks arrived all afternoon picking up and delivering weapons and ammunitions of all kinds.

HAFS was preparing for all-out war against the fae, and Sophie didn't know what to do with that information. She had the means of warning the fae queen of Iskalt, but she hesitated. At war with her heart and her mind. If she helped the fae, then it would most likely end badly for her father, and the loss of a great deal of human life. Innocents as well as those acting on hate.

But if she helped her father and HAFS, then she would lose her fae friends. She'd never see Gulliver again. And so many innocent fae lives would be destroyed for no good reason. It wasn't right.

Neither choice was one she was willing to make. So, she sat here day after day, collecting information that might help sway her one way or the other.

"Time to go back inside, Soph." Gabe sat up with a groan. "Fun time is over. I need to check in with my unit."

"Fun time, right." She set her magazine down, not having looked at a single page. Wrapping a towel around her waist, she gathered her things to go back inside.

"You're looking good, Sophie." Gabe threw an arm around her shoulders. "Strong and healthy. Whatever the doctors gave you at the hospital is really working for you."

"Sure is." Sophie pasted on a smile. Gabe was a lot like her father. He didn't want to see what was so clear to everyone else. Sophie was only here because of the kindness

Gulliver showed when he'd risked everything to save her life.

Back inside, Sophie settled on the couch in front of the TV.

"I've got to get to work." Gabe tried to pull her back up.

"Just let me catch the afternoon reports, and then your relief can take me back to my room. It's not like I'm going anywhere." She curled up against the leather sofa, tucking her beach towel around her as she turned up the volume.

"Oh, look, it's Dad." She leaned forward, eager to hear what her father had to say to the journalist interviewing him.

"It's a war on terror." Claude Devereaux said in response to the woman's question. "The fae have repeatedly brought harm to the human world, and it's time we sent them back where they belong."

"Darn right." Gabe moved to sit on the arm of the sofa next to Sophie. She cringed at his nearness, but without Gabe, she wouldn't know what was happening beyond these walls. As much as she hated to admit it, she needed him. And he was growing on her. He was as blind as her father when it came to the fae, but the difference between Claude and Gabe and the rest of HAFS was they genuinely believed they were doing the right thing.

"The fae who mistakenly believe they can claim Los Angeles for themselves will know better once we send them packing." Her father puffed up his chest and smiled into the cameras. "We're coming for you."

"We're so glad to have you here today, Mr. Devereaux. But there is one question on everyone's mind." The woman smiled into the camera, her eyes alight with curiosity. "Just where is Sophie Devereaux?"

"Hey, look at that, you're on TV." Gabe grinned. "People want to know more about you." He winked.

"My daughter is home," Claude said firmly. "That is all anyone needs to know."

"So, what are you all planning?" Sophie asked in an absent voice, like she hadn't spent the last hour working herself up to ask the simple question. She'd asked before, but Gabe was dying for her to trust him. She could sense it.

"Something big." Gabe patted her head and ran his hand down her hair.

"It sounds like Dad's planning a big battle."

"Oh, it's not just him. But it's nothing for you to worry about." He squeezed her hand. "We just want you focusing on yourself. Put your energy into your therapy sessions and getting back on your feet."

Sophie smiled and nodded. That was one thing neither of them could admit to themselves. Sophie didn't have cancer anymore. She was perfectly healthy, though they still treated her like she was made of glass.

"Some say she was healed by the fae. Is that true?" The woman on TV leaned in toward Claude.

"Uh-oh." Sophie flinched. That was the worst thing she could have asked her father.

His face turned bright red, and he shouted, "That is a lie! A filthy lie! My daughter is being treated by her doctors as we speak. She has not been tainted by fae magic." Spittle flew out of his mouth, and Sophie thought her dad looked like a lunatic. No one would ever take him seriously if he couldn't keep his temper in check.

"Touched by fae magic?" The woman frowned. "Are you saying if a fae performs magic on a human it ... taints them in some way?"

"My daughter is pure. She's a sweet girl, who has been through a lot in the last months. She needs peace and quiet."

"You let her out again, Gabe?" A HAFS soldier named

Parker sneered at Sophie. She hated Parker, but he was one of her father's trusted men and one of her regular guards.

"I needed some exercise and sunshine, Parker." Sophie sighed as she dropped the remote and stood to leave. "You may escort me back to my room." She gathered up her bag and tucked her beach towel around her waist as she followed Parker up the stairs.

"Don't expect me to give you any special treatment," Parker snapped.

"I wouldn't dream of it." Sophie waited for him to unlock the door before she stepped inside. That was her. Sophie Devereaux, willing prisoner.

"Your therapist is here." Parker opened the door to Sophie's prison room, and she forced herself to roll out of bed. Her *therapy* sessions were a joke. She didn't even think her doctor was a real doctor. He worked for HAFS and apparently specialized in people like her. Whatever that meant.

"Come on in, Doctor James." She moved to sit on the chair under the window, where they held their daily therapy sessions that usually consisted of James talking and her listening. Or pretending to listen.

"How are you feeling today, Sophie?" James sat in the chair opposite her, crossing his legs and taking out his iPad.

"Good."

"Getting plenty of rest?"

She let out a frustrated sigh. "Plenty. A lot more than I really need."

"You're still considered a cancer patient. You have to take care of yourself."

"I had new scans when I came to L.A. I feel great. Better than ever. When will I be allowed to get more exercise?"

"We want you to take it easy for now. Our sessions are part of your current treatment."

"Treatment for the crazy girl, who thinks the fae healed her cancer." Sophie smirked at the doctor pretending there was something wrong with her.

"Take me back to that day when the fae boy abducted you from your room at the hospital."

"We've been over this, Doctor. I was so sick I don't remember anything until I woke up."

"In the fae world."

"No." Sophie lied. She knew exactly what this therapy was about. The doctor wanted to know all her secrets, but she would not budge on her story. "When I woke up, I was in a nice hotel room somewhere in Los Angeles, and I felt better." She shrugged. "That is literally all I know."

"Then, why were you gone for so many months? Why did they keep you hostage?"

"No one kept me against my will. There was no one around when I woke up in that hotel room. When I asked at the desk, they said I was allowed to stay for as long as I needed. The room was paid for up to six months. So, I stayed."

"Why? Why didn't you return to your father?"

"I didn't want to." I twisted my hands in my lap. "I knew how he would react when I realized I wasn't sick anymore. And honestly, I really enjoyed not having HAFS in my life. But eventually, I got homesick, so I wanted to find my father and let him know I was okay. I didn't expect to be taken prisoner."

"You're not a prisoner, Sophie."

"I have a guard around the clock, my room is always

locked, and I'm literally not allowed to leave the grounds. Sounds like prison to me."

"It's for your own safety and health. We still need to run some tests."

"Fine, what would you like to know that I haven't already told you a dozen times?"

"Are you willing to try hypnosis?"

"Hypnosis?" Sophie gaped at the therapist. "What will that solve?"

"Sorry, Doctor," Parker stuck his head into her room, "we need to call this visit short. It seems the president is on her way, and we have to scale down our occupants to only those who absolutely have to be here."

"The HAFS president?" James tilted his head at Parker. "That doesn't make any sense."

"Because it's *the* president. Like of the United States. She'll be here within the hour, and we have to be ready."

"I see." He turned to Sophie. "Think about what I asked, and we'll talk about it next time."

"Sure." Sophie stood, just short of shooing him out of her room so she could talk to Parker. *There is no way on this earth or any other world I'm letting that charlatan hypnotize me.*

Just as Parker was about to close the door, Sophie stuck her foot out to stop him. "What's the president coming here for?" she asked.

"None of your business."

"Right. I'm sure you wouldn't know anything anyway."

"Oh, I know things. You think Claude would let one of the grunt soldiers watch over his daughter?" He scoffed, as though she'd insulted him.

"Then, what's she want with HAFS?"

"What do you think, Sophie?" He sneered. "She's finally taking us seriously. Think about it. She's coming here, to us.

That means she's ready to work with us to solve this fae problem once and for all."

Sophie frowned. "You think she's going to be on board with taking lethal action against the fae?"

"Those idiots think they can claim Los Angeles as their territory. That was an idiotic move on their part. The U.S. will not tolerate any entity on our soil who thinks they can take one of our biggest cities and we'll just sit back and let them. POTUS will take it as an act of war. Those fae creatures brought this on themselves."

"I need to see my father." She tried to push her way past Parker, but he shoved her back into the bedroom.

"He's not even here right now. He's dealing with important things. Now, be a good girl and go wash your hair or paint your fingernails."

She wanted to punch his stupid face when the click of the deadbolt sounded and she was all alone in her room again with no way of helping anyone.

Sophie paced across her room. From the big windows overlooking the pool to the bathroom and back again. There were people everywhere. HAFS people as well as the Secret Service. But Sophie couldn't think of anything other than getting to Gullie and warning him of what might be headed their way.

With the Secret Service on the grounds, now was probably not the time to try to escape. Or was it?

She peeked through the blinds of the bathroom window. Everyone was waiting for the president's arrival. They would be looking for anyone trying to sneak into the house. Not out of it.

Ever since her arrival here, she'd put off a risky attempt at escape. Her guards checked on her too often to make a go of it, and security was high during the night.

But she'd been working on a plan. If she were honest with herself, she would admit she'd just been too scared to try it. But now, she had a reason to risk it.

She could just see over the hedges to the house next door, where the landscapers were working on a new backyard. Sophie had spent hours watching them resod the backyard, adding a koi pond and a garden path from the pool to the new deck. Today, they were cleaning out the garden beds, adding new mulch, and replacing some of the wilted bushes with new flowering plants in a riot of tropical colors.

Pacing back to the bedroom, Sophie grabbed her bag. The one she kept her sunglasses and poolside reading materials in. She crouched down at the foot of her bed to retrieve Tia's journal from its hiding place under the loose floorboard and stuffed it in the bag. She hadn't written to her recently, but it was only a matter of time before she would have to.

Chewing on her bottom lip, Sophie stood in the middle of her bedroom, second-guessing herself.

"Gulliver would do it." She clutched the bag and returned to the bathroom, locking the door behind her. Climbing onto the edge of the tub, Sophie lifted the vent from the ceiling. It was a wide, industrial vent. One she'd become very familiar with over the last few weeks. At night, when everyone was sleeping, Sophie stayed up late, creeping through the vents, studying her best options for escape should it come to that.

She kept another bag in the vent with the items she'd collected to aide her escape. There was a gardening uniform she'd stolen from the basement. It looked close enough to what the landscapers next door wore that she thought she could get away with it.

After she stuffed the uniform into her bag, Sophie pulled her hair up into a hat and crawled up inside the vents, pulling it closed behind her. She shuffled her way down the hall to the second-floor laundry room. She had to psych herself up for it, but making as little noise as possible, she shimmied out of the vent, landing on top of the washing machine.

This was a mansion, and the laundry room was quite large, meant to serve as a headquarters for the maids. But HAFS didn't employ a maid service. And from what Sophie could tell, no one used the upstairs laundry room. A huge laundry chute ran down to the utility room in the basement. This was the part where she could not make any noise.

Sophie climbed feet first into the chute, letting herself slide slowly down until the shaft dropped at a sharp angle, and she lost control, landing in a heap on the concrete floor of the utility room.

And she wasn't alone. The room was full of screens showing all the security cameras on the property.

"Is that ... Sophie Devereaux?" someone asked, nudging her over with the toe of his boot. "Claude's daughter?"

Sophie looked up to find three HAFS security guards staring at her.

"I really wanted to go sit by the pool," she blurted. "Don't tell my dad."

"Come on, kid." One of the guards who couldn't have been more than a handful of years her senior pulled her up to her feet. "No one has time to deal with this right now."

"We should call Claude. He'd want to know she was trying to escape."

"She's not escaping," one of the three said. "You heard her. She just wanted to sit by the pool. Haven't you heard her guards complaining about how much she pesters them to let her out. Gabe's the only one who can control her."

"Not that I don't love hearing you all talk about me like I'm not here," Sophie gathered up her belongings and tossed her bags over her shoulder, "but either step aside and let me enjoy a few hours by the pool, or if you must, take me back to my room." She rolled her eyes and tried to pull off the spoiled dumb girl act.

"Just take her back up to Parker." The one that seemed to be in charge ordered. "I'll keep working on the cameras. Stupid Secret Service kicked us out of our own office," he muttered under his breath.

"Missing something?" The security guard marching her down the hall seemed to be taking far too much joy in her predicament.

"Sophie?" Parker glanced at the locked door and back at her. "How did you—Where have you been?" he hissed, looking over her shoulder to make sure no one else knew of his mistake.

"She was trying to get to the pool." The guard shoved her forward. "Caught her coming out of the laundry chute."

Parker snatched his keys from his pocket and unlocked the door. "Inside, now!" He pointed to her bedroom and turned on the guard. "Not a word of this to anyone. I'll handle it."

"Yes, sir." The guard gave him a salute and headed back down the hallway.

"Don't start." Sophie wiped her eyes. "I'm absolutely miserable in here, and I just wanted some fresh air."

"While the freaking President of the United States is here?" He ran a hand through his hair. "I don't know why Gabe puts up with you."

"Just leave me alone." Her eyes brightened with tears. "You don't know what it's like being cooped up in here all day."

"Save the waterworks for someone else." Parker stomped around the bedroom, checking all the windows. "How did you get out of here anyway?" He moved into the bathroom to check the windows there.

"I climbed out of the bathroom window and shimmied down to the balcony below." Sophie blew her nose loudly, amplifying her misery. "Then, I went down the hall to the laundry chute, hoping it would lead me to the back door."

"Never again, Sophie." He glared at her. "You will never do this again. At least, not on my watch."

"Don't tell my dad." She sniffed, giving Parker her best poor-me look. If he told anyone, he'd be in way more trouble than her, and he knew it.

"Just ... behave yourself, and after the president leaves, I will take you down to the pool myself." He slammed the door closed and locked her inside.

Sophie sat back on her bed, her heart hammering a mile a minute. That was close. She couldn't risk it again. At least, not for a while. She grabbed her pool bag and dragged it across the bed to her side.

There was only one thing left to do. And she should have done it long before now.

She opened the notebook and began to write.

Tia,

I've been struggling to decide what to do. But tonight, I've decided to do the right thing. There are things you need to know. Things that will help you protect the innocents on both sides of this coming war.

Because that is what this is coming to. Get the fae out of Los Angeles. They are coming for you.

And please, keep Gulliver safe.

Sophie.

Chapter Twenty-Three
GULLIVER

"The humans are coming! The humans are coming!" Griffin stumbled out of a portal into the library during the middle of a council meeting.

"Dad, are you okay?" Gulliver moved to get him a chair.

"What is he talking about?" Orla sneered at the interruption. "And does he have to do that in here?"

"When I am speaking," Griffin sucked in a breath and dropped into the chair Gulliver slid behind him, "you will listen." He gave her his fiercest, 'I'm a prince' face.

"What news do you have, uncle?" Toby gave him his full attention.

"Tia received a message from Sophie. We don't have much time."

Gulliver shot out of his chair. "How is she? Where is she?" he demanded.

"She didn't say." Griffin gave him a sympathetic look. "But she's witnessed the queen of this country arriving at the HAFS headquarters."

"You mean the president?" Xavier interjected. "The President of the United States made the effort to talk to HAFS? At their headquarters?"

"Isn't that the same thing as queen?" Griffin asked.

"Not important, but no, it's not the same." Orla tapped her dagger against the table. "Get on with it, Prince."

"War." Griffin leaned over the table. "They will bring war against us with their machines. Right here in Aghadoon."

Bedlam erupted around the room, but Griffin raised his voice. "Sophie believes it will begin after sunset ... tonight. We don't have time for bickering and mistrust." He talked over the frantic murmuring of Orla and her people. "We are all fae. Let's work together to protect our people. All of them."

"How do we know we can trust this Sophie girl?" Orla asked. "It could be a trap."

"Because she's good." Gulliver spoke without thinking. "Because she will never sit back and let innocents suffer, no matter what blood they carry in their veins. I'd stake my life on her word. And Tia's. Tierney O'Shea is not stupid. She would have tested the messenger to make sure the person writing in the journal was no one other than Sophie-Ann Devereaux. We would be fools to even consider this warning is any sort of trap. It's our chance to prepare, and we shouldn't waste any more time."

"Put out the call," Orla issued the command to her right hand. He gave a nod and quickly left to gather his unit.

"What call?" Toby asked, looking at Xavier for answers.

"We have to protect the fae of Los Angeles," Orla answered, holding up a hand to halt her people from leaving. "Since our arrival in Los Angeles, we've established safe houses throughout the city. Old bunkers, basements, and shelters where our fae can go to escape attacks like the one we face now. Each shelter will have magic wielders capable of erecting minor shields of protection, though our magic is nothing compared to yours."

"Grandfather?" Toby turned to Brandon. "Do we have any soldiers to spare for these shelters?"

"Come with me to Fargelsi for an hour, and we will have a team of magic wielders for each shelter. You are the only O'Shea able to accomplish such a feat in time."

Toby exchanged a look with Xavier before he nodded. "Let's go." He left with Brandon, and a moment later Gulliver saw the flash of Toby's portal through the window.

"Aghadoon will open its doors to anyone needing refuge tonight." Orla's eyes blazed with defiance, as if anyone would disagree with her.

"Of course." Griffin nodded. "As the senior royal representative of the fae world in Brandon's absence, I give you my word we will not turn away anyone with even a drop of fae blood. But when the battle is upon us, our shields will go up and our doors will be sealed. Make sure your fae know the time to act is now. Anyone within an hour's distance from the village will be welcome with open arms. Others will need to seek refuge elsewhere."

"Cal, let everyone know help is on the way," Orla said. Her soldier went to deliver the message.

"Do we know anything more?" Xavier asked. "Is that all Sophie said?"

"The humans and their leader didn't like it when Toby declared Los Angeles a safe haven for fae," Griffin said. "The human queen saw it as the fae's attempt to take territory away from this country. She took it as an act of war."

"That's not what he meant," Gulliver said. "He just wanted the fae to have a central, safe place where we could protect them."

"What we meant doesn't matter," Orla said as she stood. "And we don't have time for further discussion. Can my fae treat Aghadoon as our center of command during the fight?"

"Of course," Griffin said. "We are here to help."

"Your *help* was what got us into this mess."

"And we'll help get us all out of it." Gulliver moved to stand beside his father at the table.

"I will ask that your fae take charge of protecting Aghadoon," Orla said. "But mine will be in charge of this battle as a whole."

"Agreed." Griffin nodded. "Our soldiers and magic wielders are here to help, but outside of Aghadoon, you are in charge."

Orla scowled at Griffin. "I remember you. Weren't you the buffoon who got the media's attention in a taco outing with your son just a few days ago?"

"Yes, but I am also a Prince of Iskalt and guardian of the rift in Myrkur. When the time calls for it, I can be a ruler. It took me a long time to learn to embrace life with my family to its fullest. I prefer a life with little responsibility, but make no mistake, I am no imbecile when it comes to war."

"Noted." Orla lifted her chin, showing the first signs of respect for him.

Toby and Brandon returned within the hour with both Lenyan and Gelsi soldiers and magic wielders. Even Gulliver could understand the strategy there. No one wanted the humans to learn how their magic worked. That Iskaltians only had magic at night, while Eldurians were powerful during the day. And Myrkurians only had defensive magic.

With Fargelsians and Lenyans, there were no limitations to when they could use their magic. The Gelsi soldiers would draw their power from the ancient words of magic and from the earth itself, while Lenyans held powerful totems to direct their magic. With Brandon and Griffin in charge of the night battle, the village's vulnerabilities were safe for the moment.

"We have Eldurians and a fresh troop of Lenyans gathered in Iskalt should we need them," Toby explained when he returned with his grandfather. "I'll go back just before dawn if the fight still continues. Uncle Finn and Keir will return with me to relieve Griffin and Brandon."

Gulliver paced across the library, unsure of how much help he would be in this fight when he had no magic to speak of. Gripping the sword at his hip, he knew he could protect himself with it, but it was the only weapon he was good at.

"Why so frustrated?" Griffin found him walking the dusty aisles of the library. "Besides the obvious worry about the coming battle and that your girl is out there somewhere with the enemy."

"She's not my girl." Gulliver shrugged. "But I still worry about her. She's my friend."

"And she's a smart young lady. She can handle her father." Griffin laid a hand on Gulliver's arm. "Promise me you won't go galivanting across this topsy-turvy city tonight trying to save her?"

"I don't even know where she is." Gullie sighed, turning toward the wide windows facing the activity swarming at the center of Aghadoon. "And I'm not much good to anyone here."

"You will lead the company charged with protecting the library."

"What?" Gulliver's head snapped toward his father. "Are you *insane*? Shouldn't that responsibility fall to Brandon?"

Griffin chuckled and shook his head. “Brandon’s magic will be needed elsewhere tonight. But Aghadoon is a sacred place. You know what it would mean for our people should it be destroyed.”

Gulliver nodded, his tail thumping against the floor with a nervous tick.

“And if the library itself should need to be protected, that would mean the humans have breached our shields and our magic wielders have fallen.”

Gulliver nodded again. “I will protect the magic of Aghadoon with my life.”

“No, you will not.” Griffin smiled. “You will protect it to the best of your ability, but haven’t we all learned an important lesson over the years? Magic isn’t everything. It’s a huge part of our way of life, but we can live without it if we have to.”

“You’re right. I live without magic all the time, and I’m okay.” Gulliver gave his father a half smirk.

“Be careful tonight, son.” Griffin pulled him into his arms.

“You too, Dad. We’ve been through a lot, you and me. From the slums of the Myrkur palace to the happy life we had for a short time in Fela before we met Mom.”

“That’s when all our adventures began.” Griffin laughed at the memory of those days. “I’ll be helping Brandon guard the walls of the village,” Griffin said as they broke apart. “If you need anything, send a messenger.”

“Good luck, Dad.” Gulliver slapped him on the back. “If you get hurt, Mom’s going to kill you.”

“Don’t I know it.” Griffin smiled as he left the library to take up his position for the attack.

“I still haven’t seen any signs of the human army yet.” Toby peeked out the windows after Griffin left.

"You'd think if they planned to attack us at sunset, they'd have their soldiers in place by now." Gulliver returned to his pacing.

"From what Orla has told me, the humans prefer the element of surprise." Toby walked in the opposite direction of Gulliver.

"We should see their funny bird planes soon."

"Helicopters," Toby supplied. "Xavier said we will be fine with our shields up." Toby fidgeted restlessly in front of the large window overlooking the park with the Hollywood sign in clear view. "I just don't know why he has to go out there without me."

"We don't have magic," Gulliver said sadly.

"Neither does he. Not much anyway." Toby sighed. "He can protect himself with basic shields, but that's as much magic as he has. But he insisted on going out to help bring his people to safety."

"Then, what are we doing here where it's safe?" Gulliver stared off across the city, wondering where Sophie was and if she would be safe tonight.

"We are doing what royals always do." Toby sighed. "We give the orders and plan the strategies our soldiers will execute because that is what they have been trained to do, and this is what we have been trained to do."

"Yeah, but I'm not royal."

Toby reached for Gulliver's hand. "You're royal adjacent. Everyone knows you belong with me and Tia."

"Thanks, Tobes." Gulliver gave his hand a squeeze.

"It's nearly sunset," Toby said. "We should probably get ready to take our positions outside." Toby was responsible for helping Gulliver protect the library that would likely never need to be protected. But Toby had to be ready to open a large enough portal to evacuate fae should the need arise.

"Send out the message to the Google man," Toby said. "Then, let's go."

"It's not Google, Toby." Gulliver sat down at the table and took Xavier's tablet in hand. "It's the ClockTok." He tapped on the icon and hit record like Xavier showed him. "Hi there, internet people. This message is for all the fae of Los Angeles and the surrounding areas." He read from the script Xavier had left for him. "Do not be alarmed. The humans have decided they don't want us to be safe here in the city. Most of you know this by now as the message has been going out to all the local fae communities since early this afternoon. The humans plan to attack us at any moment. If you have not already arrived at a safehouse, stay wherever you are. If you can get to a basement, lock up your house and seek shelter in place. Do not go outside. I repeat. No matter what you hear, do not go outside. My people and our trained soldiers and magic wielders will protect you. Stay safe, and if you are anywhere near the Hollywood Hills, no matter what you hear, stay in your homes. HashtagBeSafe."

"No, you type the hashtags, Gullie!" Toby hissed.

"Oh, right sorry. I'll hashtag you all in a minute. Be safe." Gulliver ended the video and copied all the text Xavier had written out for him before he posted the video.

Gulliver heard a deep humming noise that reverberated in his chest.

"They're coming." Toby double checked the sword at his hip.

"Let's go."

They crossed the library and exited onto the porch of the rundown building that was older than anyone would ever know. Gulliver felt an overwhelming urge to protect it and all the magical secrets it held within.

Toby took half their unit to guard the front of the

building and Gulliver took the other half to the rear, where Aghadoon overlooked the Hollywood Hills. Nothing stood between him and the fast human planes flying overhead but a wide field of grass and the glow of magic sealing the village off from anything the humans might throw at them.

"All right, soldiers." Gulliver faced his troops. All eight of them. "We might not have the most dangerous task tonight, and we may very well end up with a front row seat to a quick and easy battle, but we are guarding one of the most important artifacts known to faekind. Do not take it lightly. Stay on alert, and should it come to a fight, give it your all, but when I say enough is enough, we will abandon the village if the call is given."

"Yes, sir!" The young rag-tag group of half-fae and a few young Fargelsians drew their weapons and prepared for a long night.

"Gelsi soldiers, get your shields up."

"Yes, sir!" The two magic wielders he'd been given went to work, calling out their Gelsi spells to weave a web or protective magic over the library, independent of the stronger shields over the village.

"That was so weird," Gulliver muttered to himself, wondering how on earth he'd ended up leading even these few soldiers all on his own.

A sharp whistling noise had them alert and on guard a moment later.

"What is that?" a Gelsi soldier asked, looking up to the sky for a source of the noise.

"Bombs," a half-fae from New Orleans answered. "I sure hope your magic is as strong as you all claim." His hands trembled as he lifted his weapon—a human automatic gun.

"Keep your focus soldier," one of his fellow half-fae soldiers said, her own voice shaking.

"I've seen magic shields strong enough to isolate an entire kingdom," Gulliver reassured them. But even he couldn't take his eyes away from the glaze of magic in all colors surrounding them.

"That one sounds close!" A girl from Gelsi looked at Gulliver for orders. "What do we do, My Lord?"

"Stay in place." Gulliver gripped his weapon, feeling frustrated that there wasn't an obvious enemy to fight.

The ground shook beneath them, and something exploded overhead.

"What's happening?" Gulliver crouched, throwing his hands over his head, but nothing rained down on top of them.

"It's working!" The Gelsi soldiers cheered.

"What was that?" Gulliver moved away from the protection of the building, down onto the grassy slopes behind Aghadoon. The sky was alight with bursts of colors in every shade, but nothing breached the shields.

"A bomb just exploded right freaking there." One of the half-fae soldiers moved to stand beside him. "And it just stopped in dead air. Like magic." She turned in a circle, staring up at the sky.

"That *was* magic." Gulliver let out a whoop of joy, relieved that the shields seemed to be holding. For now.

Chapter Twenty-Four
SOPHIE-ANN

"Gabe!" Sophie hammered on the door to her room, but no one came. It had been that way for hours.

"Ugh, I'm sick of this." She pushed away from the door, rubbing the side of her hand. Something was going on. Something big, and Tia was counting on her for information.

She didn't have a choice. Sophie gathered up her nerve and her bag and headed for the bathroom. She hadn't tried escaping again, but she had figured out where she could hide in the vent systems to overhear conversations.

One of those was the common room just down the hall from her bedroom. Close enough where she could get back quickly if she saw anyone coming up the stairs or heading for her room, but far enough where she could see what was going on throughout the house.

Turning on the shower to cover her absence, she pulled herself up into the vent and inched her way toward the nearest the common room. Instantly, she noticed a difference.

On a normal day, HAFS members swarmed all over the house, gathering in multiple rooms to hold meetings and discussions.

Today, the house was quiet. Only a few members could be seen from her vantage point. One of them was her father and a man she didn't recognize. Seated beside the cold fireplace, they talked quietly as others came and went up and down the stairs on their various errands.

"How are her therapy sessions going with Doctor James?" the older man asked her father.

"He says she's receptive to what he has to say, but he feels her resistance whenever he brings up hypnotic therapy."

"Because it's not happening with that quack," Sophie murmured to herself. *If he's an actual doctor, I'm a super model.* She crept forward, inching toward the vent closest to the fireplace, where she could hear them better. She could also see the news on the giant television, and it caught her attention for a moment when she saw the fae village that had settled in the Hollywood Hills. Her thoughts drifted to Gulliver, and she hoped he had safely returned to Iskalt.

That thought gave her courage.

"You know what she needs," the man sitting with her father said. "You're just prolonging the inevitable."

"I want her treated right here where I can keep an eye on her," Claude insisted.

"In Sophie's situation, one-on-one therapy will only get her so far." The man leaned forward, elbows on his knees as he talked with her father. "She has a long way to go, Claude. She's been touched by fae magic. We know that for certain now."

Sophie let out a small gasp. They were talking about her cancer. She knew she was healed and cancer free, but it was still hard to believe.

"All her scans are clear. The doctors can't find a single thing wrong with her. None of the usual minor abnormalities that come up in routine MRIs. No inflammation in her abdomen from the chemotherapy. Claude, there are no signs the girl ever had cancer treatment of any kind, much less just months ago. If the clinical trial healed her like you insist, then her body would be wrecked by the drugs. She'd still be weak and struggling to recover her stamina. Whatever they did to her while she was in fae captivity, it restored her body to its fullest. She is the picture of health."

"And I'm glad for it." Claude hung his head, and his shoulders shook with silent sobs. "What does that say about me, Doctor?"

The doctor reached over to rest a hand on Claude's back. "It says you're a good father, who is grateful to have his daughter whole again. But she will always hold the taint of their magic within her. We need to take her in for the full treatment."

"I know." Her father wiped his tears away. Sophie had never seen him cry. Even at her mother's funeral, Claude Devereaux was a pillar of strength for his daughter.

"I don't want things to end for Sophie the way they did for her mother."

Claude's eyes snapped up to glare at the doctor. "I did what was expected of me. I did everything your father asked, and it didn't work."

"And my father and I both tried to help her, but she didn't want it. She was too far gone. Sophie isn't."

"I'm scared for my little girl." Claude twisted his hands in his lap, not meeting the other man's eyes.

"Sophie isn't in love with this fae boy who took her to his world. She doesn't show any of the signs her mother displayed when she came back to you."

What are they talking about? Sophie pressed her ear toward the vent, trying not to miss a word of their conversation. Nothing they'd said about her mother made any sense. She was killed in a fae attack.

"And that is a relief, but I'm still hesitant to let her go to that place. When my wife came back, she wasn't the same."

"And it was her own fault. She didn't do the work. She resisted the therapy. In the end, you had no choice but to end her life."

Sophie nearly cried out but slammed a hand over her mouth, her eyes wide with disbelief.

"It was the hardest thing I've ever done. I loved my wife. Even after she ran off with that filthy fae monster, who convinced her she didn't love me anymore."

Mom cheated? With a fae? Sophie wracked her brain, but she couldn't remember a time when her mother wasn't there. Not until after her death.

"Like mother, like daughter," the doctor said. "But it's not too late for Sophie. Not yet. I don't want to see her executed like her mother."

Sophie clamped her mouth shut, choking back her sobs as her heart broke into a thousand tiny pieces. Her mother hadn't died because of a fae attack. She'd died because she'd fallen in love with a fae. And HAFS killed her for it.

"It would kill me to see that happen to her." Claude sobbed. "I took care of her mother. It was my responsibility to see it done, but I could never end my daughter's life." He shook his head. "I'd rather die myself than see her end up like her mother."

"Then, the only choice is to let us take her, Claude. She needs our full attention. Together, we can erase the damage the fae have done to her mind and body, but we must act soon or we'll lose our chance to help her."

Claude nodded. "I will tell her tomorrow."

Good luck with that, Dad. Because I will not be here. She didn't care what it took. Tonight, while the house was quieter than usual, she was out of here. Sophie started to inch her way back toward her room when Gabe darted up the stairs into the common room.

"It's started." He grabbed the remote and turned up the volume. "Their magic is proving to be strong. We haven't been able to penetrate their shields yet, but the president has given orders to shower their strongholds with everything the air force has."

Sophie wiped her tears and turned her focus on the screen. Fires had erupted all over Los Angeles. She watched as bombs rained down on the fae village, exploding against the dome of magic the fae had erected to protect themselves.

Sophie breathed a sigh of relief that they were safe. At least, for the moment.

Her father and the doctor leapt out of their seats a moment later, blocking the screen from her. "Would you look at that?" Claude whistled, all his emotions over his daughter vanished in his excitement for the war he'd had a hand in starting. "It's cracking."

"We'll get through those shields yet." Gabe slapped Claude on the back. "Wish I could be out there fighting the good fight."

"You will, son." Claude draped an arm around him. "This is just the beginning. Before it's over with, the armed forces will be begging for HAFS soldiers. We've been fighting fae scum for more than a decade."

They moved, and Sophie caught a glimpse of the huge screen again. Chaos rained down on the fae. They'd managed to breach the shields and some of the old buildings were burning. A lone figure stood on the slopes behind the village, waving his sword toward the sky. She'd know him anywhere.

"Gullie." She gasped just before another bomb lit up the sky. The explosion broke through the barrier, and there was too much smoke and fire to see if the boy she owed her life to was still there.

"I gotta go check on Sophie. Make sure she's not up to anything." Gabe snickered as he headed toward her door.

"Crap." She shuffled back down the vent as quickly as she dared.

"Hold off on that," Claude called him back. "I need to talk to her first." Sophie couldn't hear them anymore as she dove through the vent in her bathroom, landing in the tub with a hard smack against the surface. "Ouch." She scrambled up and slammed the vent shut.

Her heart was still hammering in her chest as she leaped onto her bed and picked up a book from her bedside table just as the door opened.

"Hey." She glanced up, expecting to see her father with Gabe, but the doctor stood in the middle of the room with two guards she didn't recognize. "Oh, I'm sorry." She closed her book with trembling hands. "I was expecting Gabe."

"Hi there, Sophie. I'm Doctor Clarkson. I've been speaking with your father about your therapy." It was then she realized she'd met him before. The commander.

"I see." She dropped her gaze to the floor. She didn't trust herself not to start screaming and raging about everything she'd just overheard.

"You aren't making enough progress under Doctor James. Claude understands your health is of the utmost importance."

"And what do you suggest, Doctor?" Sophie willed herself to remain calm. She needed to agree to whatever the doctor said just to appease him enough to leave her alone for the night. She had to get out of here immediately before it was too late.

"I have a new treatment I'd like to give you tonight. It's just a mild sedative that will help you relax and open your mind." He turned to one of the guards, who handed him a pill bottle. "Nothing scary, I promise." He gave her a fake smile and handed her two yellow pills.

"What is this for?"

"It's part of your treatment. Your father has signed off on it."

"I'm an adult. I make my own decisions for my health." She knew it sounded lame given that she was standing inside the prison cell her father had locked her in for weeks.

"Not this time, Sophie, dear. You've gone through a traumatic experience with the fae. It's important that you trust us to take care of you."

"I'm fine. Perfectly healthy." *You said so yourself, you lousy creep.*

"You're dealing with residual issues that can't always be seen on the surface."

"Is this part of some kind of hypnosis therapy? Because I've told *Doctor* James a million times I'm not doing that."

"We can talk about it." The doctor approached her.

Sophie scooted back, and the guards descended on her. One of them held her down, and the doctor swooped in and stuck something in her arm.

"Ouch!" Sophie pressed a hand over her arm as the guards eased their grip on her.

The room started to spin, and her world went dark. Her last conscious thought was that she'd left Tia's journal in the vents.

Sophie woke up with a pounding headache and stars dancing overhead.

Her vision cleared, and she realized she was seeing the actual stars. But she couldn't move. Her arms and legs were strapped down, and someone wheeled her on a gurney toward a set of double doors.

"What's happening?" Her words came out slurred, and her head felt as though it weighed a hundred pounds.

"Shh, Sophie, everything will be all right," a stranger's voice sounded just behind her. "We'll get you settled into your room in a jiffy, and you'll be able to rest soon."

"Where am I?" She blinked her eyes as the man rolled her toward those doors. "No. Stop." She tried to move, but the man kept pushing the gurney.

"No. Don't take me in there." Panic rose in her chest as she made out the sign above the door.

Welcome to the Clarkson Institute.

Epilogue

"August, where are you going?" The nurse chased after the rambunctious ten-year-old.

"I have to see." He avoided her grasp and ran for the windows. That burning sensation he got from time to time was stronger. He could feel it pulsing just under his skin. The doctor didn't like it when he talked about how powerful the sensation made him feel.

"August, stop it this instant."

"I just want to see her." He hopped up on the table at the end of the common room, pressing his face against the windows. So many times, he'd wanted to break through that glass and leave the institute behind, but he wasn't strong enough. And there was no one out there who could help him anyway. Instead, he watched as the girl on the gurney twisted and turned, trying to free herself of the restraints. He wanted to tell her that was the last thing she should do. They would just give her the yellow pills that would make her sleep all day and drool on herself.

"The girl with the blue hair," he whispered, his breath fogging up the glass. "She's real."

"Who is she?" The nurse took his arm and pulled him back down from the table. "How do you know anything about this girl, August?"

What she meant was, how could he possibly know anything about a girl he'd never seen before when he'd never set a foot outside this building in his whole life.

"She's the one I've been waiting for."

There's one more book to finish up the series!
Fae's End is available now!

About Melissa

Melissa A. Craven is an Amazon bestselling author of Young Adult Contemporary Fiction and YA Fantasy (her Contemporary fans will know her as Ann Maree Craven). Her books focus on strong female protagonists who aren't always perfect, but they find their inner strength along the way. Melissa's novels appeal to audiences of all ages and fans of almost any genre. She believes in stories that make you think and she loves playing with foreshadowing, leaving clues and hints for the careful reader.

Melissa draws inspiration from her background in architecture and interior design to help her with the small details in world building and scene settings. (Her degree in fine art also comes in handy.) She is a diehard introvert with a wicked sense of humor and a tendency for hermit-like behavior. (Seriously, she gets cranky if she has to put on anything other than yoga pants and t-shirts!)

Melissa enjoys gardening and sitting on her porch when the weather is nice with her two dogs, Fynlee and Nahla, reading from her massive TBR pile and dreaming up new stories.

Visit Melissa at Melissaacraven.com for more information about her newest series and discover exclusive content.

Want to see more books by Melissa A. Craven? You can view them here

Join Melissa and Michelle's Facebook Group: Fantasy Book Warriors

About Michelle

Michelle MacQueen is a USA Today bestselling author of love. Yes, love. Whether it be YA romance, NA romance, or fantasy romance (Under M. Lynn), she loves to make readers swoon.

The great loves of her life to this point are two tiny blond creatures who call her "aunt" and proclaim her books to be "boring books" for their lack of pictures. Yet, somehow, she still manages to love them more than chocolate.

When she's not sharing her inexhaustible wisdom with her niece and nephew, Michelle is usually lounging in her ridiculously large bean bag chair creating worlds and characters that remind her to smile every day - even when a feisty five-year-old is telling her just how much she doesn't know.

See more from M. Lynn and sign up
to receive updates and deals!
michellelynnauthor.com

Join Melissa and Michelle's Facebook Group:
Fantasy Book Warriors
Follow Michelle and Melissa on TikTok
@ATaleOfTwoAuthors
Want to see more books by Michelle?
visit https://books2read.com/ap/R5my46/M-Lynn

More From Brea's World

Don't miss the FREE prequel,
Fae's Dilemma
Grab your copy here!

www.ingramcontent.com/pod-product-compliance
Lightning Source LLC
Chambersburg PA
CBHW030530310726
48979CB00010B/1863/J

* 9 7 8 1 9 7 0 0 5 2 9 0 9 *